ROBERT F.B. HANSBROUGH

Desperate Journey

When We Were Young & The Great Depression

Order this book online at www.trafford.com/07-0656
or email orders@trafford.com

Most Trafford titles are also available at major online book retailers.

Note for Librarians: A cataloguing record for this book is available from Library and Archives Canada at www.collectionscanada.ca/amicus/index-e.html

ISBN: 978-1-4251-2255-3

We at Trafford believe that it is the responsibility of us all, as both individuals and corporations, to make choices that are environmentally and socially sound. You, in turn, are supporting this responsible conduct each time you purchase a Trafford book, or make use of our publishing services. To find out how you are helping, please visit www.trafford.com/responsiblepublishing.html

Our mission is to efficiently provide the world's finest, most comprehensive book publishing service, enabling every author to experience success. To find out how to publish your book, your way, and have it available worldwide, visit us online at www.trafford.com/10510

www.trafford.com

North America & international
toll-free: 1 888 232 4444 (USA & Canada)
phone: 250 383 6864 • fax: 250 383 6804 • email: info@trafford.com

The United Kingdom & Europe
phone: +44 (0)1865 722 113 • local rate: 0845 230 9601
facsimile: +44 (0)1865 722 868 • email: info.uk@trafford.com

10 9 8 7 6 5

"Desperate Journey—
When We Were Young & The Great Depression"

Life is a series of journeys, laced with smiles, tears, hopes, & sorrows.
This is the story of some of them.

CONTENTS

ALSO BY THE AUTHOR

I Completed:

WWII Memories—BB-64 © 1987

Self Published by Author; Promoted by the U.S. Naval Institute.

Memories of WWII on one of the largest battleships in the world.

Adventures of Clarice © 1991

Sailing Adventures on the 24' Trimaran, "Clarice," and on the 35' Ketch, "Clarice II," both built by the author & named after his dear wife, Clarice, who sailed with him on many an interesting adventure on both the great lakes and the waters of Puget Sound and the British Columbia coast.

"Navigation Manual, Piloting & Offshore for the Small Boat Sailor." © 1994.

All you really need to know to "find your way around" on the inland seas and great oceans. With emphasis on time proven simple techniques.

Also, a first hand account of a harrowing "blow" on Lake St. Clair in a 24-foot Trimaran just off its heavily traveled freighter lanes on a batten breaking stormy night, and what it was like to be in the middle of "the greatest storm in recorded history" on the battleship *U.S.S. Wisconsin*-BB-64 during those very anxious WWII times with our engulfed 3rd fleet as we struggled to survive the raging elements of nature as they tried to "do us in." (Three destroyers didn't make it!) All who survived felt very fortunate indeed!

Note: The author was a senior C.E.M. (acting) in the U.S. Navy; held a chief electricians licence in the Merchant Marines and had a master's licence (O.U.P.V.) from the U.S. Coast Guard.

II In Process

"A Sailor's Tales—WWII & India" © R.F.H.

A few untold sea stories of WWII on the fleet minesweeper *U.S.S. Motive*-A.M.-102 and battleship *U.S.S. Wisconsin*-BB-64. Also a most historic adventure filled trip to the :\"Far East" on *the S.S. Seaphoenix* (C3 type cargo ship owned by the Isthmian Steamship Co.) during those very politically & religiously unsettled years of the mid-to-late '40's. I was the chief electrician and watched many dramatic, historic events unfold.

"The Best of Times; The Worst of Times—Chances are You're Next" © R.F.H.

A very personal, kowing story of what it is like to find you and your loved ones are suddenly "old" and in the clutches of a governmentally controlled care and medical system that fails us all.

"How Proudly We Served" © R.F.H.

Anecdotes of service in WWII, particularly on the new fleet mine sweeper U.S.S. Motive A.M.-102 in the Aleutians when it was still occupied by the Japanese.

Includes: Study & preparation prior to commissioning; under enemy fire (bombers from Paramushir) at Attu; A great gale and a little ship: riding out a great gale with a fellow sailor on a mooring buoy for hours during a long, dark night in Massacre Bay, Attu. Also, fighting a raging oil-fed fire in the forward engine room alone with a 2" hose and fog nozzle. I was beginning to lose my solitary battle when a fire & rescue party from the tanker U.S.S. Neches, sailed over the waves in their whale boat to join me and save the ship. The damage was so extensive we went back on one screw for repairs in the States.

R.F.H.

DEDICATION

To Our Precious Clarice
Whose Beautiful Memory
Shall Never Die.

Bob

Acknowledgments

* Those who also played a big part in this story.

Very special thanks to those who were there for Clarice in her time of need. Her eyes lit up when she heard their steps coming and she smiled all the while they were near.

Anne Clarice Deer

Held Clarice in her arms as she was dying: "We love you, mom—it's OK to leave." And with a tiny little sound to say "goodbye," she flew away. Dear Lord, please hold her gently in your arms. We loved her so!

Don Hansbrough

Visited "Mom" the hard way. Often by foot, ferry and bus.

Beth & David Kryger.

Drove miles upon miles from across "the sound" then miles after that to bring "Mom" cheer.

***Amy Karleen "Sis" Hodson**

Came time after time from a long ways away to be with her cherished big sister.

Cal White

Our very special minister who visited often to join us in prayer.

Vicki and Ray Kobeski

Very dear young friends who visited often and brought so much cheer.

Lois Bays

Vicki's mother who was often there by our sides to give us courage.

Ted Ballew

A dear sailor friend from "way back." As we were with him to say goodbye to his dear Fayetta, so was he with me to say adieu to my darling Clarice.

Others who were there at the end to say goodbye:

Gerry Fulkrod, Charles & *Roxanne Hodson, Rob & Carrie Hodson, David & Sue Hodson, Lois Johnson, Fred & Pam Levin, Nathan & Natalie Kryger, Raymond C. Lewis Jr., Burt & *Sandy Peterson, Jeff & Tammy Peterson, Eric & Karen Peterson, Dan & Linda Poort, Ava Waits, Sammy Waits, Madeline Waits, Woody Waits & *Ardyce Wolfe.

Others who played a big part in the info for this story:

My sister Marjory and her husband, Norman Chaviers of the Appalachians; Theresa "Terry" Vanderley; my dear little sister, Janie Carson, who has written me such beautiful letters; cousin Elsie Deutsch in Kentucky who has kept in touch through all of the years.

And a very heart-felt thanks to the following dear friends:

Jerold "Jerry" W. Oliver & Lorraine Thiel, classmates of '42 at T.C.H.S.—Traverse City Michigan. What wonderful friends they have been to me over the many years!

As the national President of a construction organization, Jerry once met and flew on a private jet with the then future president, Ronald Reagan. Lorraine was, for a long time. A lead "string" in a Northern Michigan Symphony Orchestra. We still plan to meet together as long as the Good Lord will allow it to be.

To John Picuri and Steve Umina, old WWII shipmates on the battleship *U.S.S. Wisconsin*-BB-64, who laid wreaths on the waters by our old ship (now a museum at Norfolk, Virginia) in the memory of Clarice. For this and their many kindnesses, I will never forget!

To Margaret "Peggy" Aaronson who patiently, understandingly listened for hours to this story during its formulation and helped me through the most difficult, saddest days of my life!

Not often in a lifetime are we blessed with such wonderful friends!

Robert F.B. Hansbrough

As the Years Go By

By Edgar A. Guest
(From "A Song for Today")

We plan and work for
Years of bliss.
And Peace and quite and
Delight
Yet there are loved ones
We may miss,
Before the coming of the
Night.
We pay for age with pain and tears,
And loneliness to still to
Bear.
We buy with grief a few
More years,
To look upon a vacant
Chair.
But as the book of memories
Glows.
We turn the pages,
And are glad
And grateful for the joys
It shows.
And all the love that
We have had.

Copied from some of his old memories
by Bob (2006)

Introduction

Desperate Journey—When We Were Young & The Great Depression.

THIS IS really two stories in one whose backgrounds and recitations are inalterable mingled.

One is the story of the "Great Depression," the why's and wherefores of it's happening and the lessons staring us in our faces, that could prevent or minimize it ever again happening, should we, the inheritors of this wonderful land, with all of its promise, choose to take a little "time-out" and listen.

The other—The most precious, poignant to me—is a series of little anecdotes about the dear ones of my extended family—The Peterson's, the Vanderley's, the Weenums, the Poort's and many others, including my own who were there at the time, doing their very best to survive—and do so in dignity and with the love and care for their fellow man—during those long ago, horrible, heart-breaking times.

Throughout this story, I have drawn heavily on my own experiences and the experiences and recollections of dear family members and friends who were there, in the middle of "things" when they happened.

As I've said many times before: I am such a very fortunate person to have been in their company!

Robert F. (Bob) Hansbrough.

PART ONE

When We Were Young

CHAPTER IA

Sunday Dinner at the Petersons

I AM 82 years old now going on 83—and am, so to speak, a veritable remnant of a fast vanishing herd of later day "dinosaurs."

Let me start out by telling you a little about those "good old days" of the waning years of the "Great Depression." Those days when I first met Bill and Myrtle Peterson and their wonderful, young, growing up family.

I was a young lad in my very early twenties in those days, recently returned from the battles in the South Pacific and my first semester at the University of Michigan.

I was alive. The day was beautiful. I had been just invited again for Sunday dinner by the Petersons at their home on Burton Road! My best friend, Ralph Vanderley and his pretty wife, Teresa (Terry) would be probably there waiting. And Clarice just might be home again from teaching in South Haven!

Then closing the door to my cozy little rental room on Webster St., I hurried down the stairs to my '36 Chevy, pumped on the accelerator a few times, stepped on the starter button and headed that way.

It was sure to be a wonderful day. And looking back in memory, it certainly was!

What wonderful times I was privileged to share in my day!

What beautiful, precious friends!

Then, after re-parking my car on the gravel side driveway (the garage with its little attached apartment wouldn't be built by Sam Werner for a number of years yet), handsome, smiling brother Bob with his wavy blond hair quickly walked in. And we all bowed our head in prayer while mother said Grace.

Then the steaming bowls of mashed potatoes and gravy and roast beef and goodies of all description quickly make the rounds. And, in between the mouthfuls and smiles of appreciation, the joyous chattering began. And seemingly never ended. And still continues in beautiful memory, in the hearts of those still with us today!

And, yes! My beautiful, wonderful Claire *was* there! Happy and gregarious as ever and glowing in the radiance of the friendship and love and care that exuded from all around. (We were married a few years later. And now she's in heaven!) I'll never, ever forget! All of the rest of the sisters and brothers were there too. And each had a tale of their own to tell:

Attractive, bubbly Ardyce had just signed up at Central State in Mount Pleasant and was going to become a teacher. She was looking forward to the new adventure.

Tall, good-looking, easy-going brother Burt was there too, just enjoying the summer vacation from Muskegon High, fishing in "The Channel" and on nearby lakes, swimming when he got the chance. Working at odd jobs when he could find them. In all reality, just enjoying the ambience of the times and the friendship of friends and family.

Burt always was (and still is) very good at playing the baritone.

In those beautiful early days, when Claire was still with us, she and I would go, once in a while, to a Muskegon High football game to enjoy the rivalry and watch Burt, and his "Big Reds" band as they proudly, saucily, swing and swayed up and down the field before us, to the stirring tune and cadence of "The Stars and Stripes Forever," and other snappy, catchy patriotic songs.

Boy, what wonderful days those were!

It seems that Burt was always interested in the beauty and the nature of things all around us. But, not only did he "look" to revel in their beauty, he searched to find the essence of that beauty and discover how it could be recaptured and recreated in other forms—perhaps by simply the use of a lot of thought, and a lot of pencil-wearing on the drawing board—for a multitude of "practical" uses (some mundane and some very dramatic) such as the practice of architecture, automobile design and fabrication, layout of cities, and the design of machines and equipment that would make those all possible.

Burt chose the latter. And he was good at it! And his skills and knowledge of what he did, and his friendly, cooperative ways in the doing, were widely known. And his work was in much demand.

Take a look today at the inside walls of Burt's garage that are covered with his paintings (for sure, the influence of Disney and his animated characters played a big part there) and you'll get a sense of the creative bent (and art ability) that has never left and is still with him.

Take a stroll through the beautiful, well-appointed rooms in his home and I'm sure you'll be impressed!

Open a door down the hallway to a nearby room. Inside you'll find a well-used drawing board, and accompanying stool to sit on, and an array of well used pencils, triangles, measuring scales (and the like) and you'll suddenly discover you are on the site of his "doing."

But let's hold on now! Burt had plenty of encouragement and her name is Sandra ("Sandy" to all of us). She is one of the strikingly beautiful (in looks and character) Weenum sisters. Claire and I were at their wedding many years ago! And she was a teacher too, just like Claire. And for many years, Sandy and Burt were some of our very best friends. And thought Claire is now gone, I cherish their friendship and love today even more.

Ralph Vanderley, my best friend from high school (Traverse City, Michigan) and his charming young wife Teresa ("Terry" to us) had driven down from Traverse City with their three-year-old son, Bobby to join us on this really special occasion. "Special" because Ralph's work up north in his brother's business didn't allow much movement from that area this time of year. "Very special" because Terry was "expecting" another baby soon! And they had to stay close to home as much as they could before and after that wonderful event!

And speaking of "special,' their presence was that to me too! In a number of ways.

Ralph and I had lived not far from each other during some of the worst times of those difficult Depression years.

We had shared the meals at each other's homes when there wasn't much to eat. And had walked to school in the same kinds of worn-out shoes and patched-up clothes. And we often shivered to sleep in the same cold, cold nights when there wasn't enough chopped up mill-wood or scrounged-up lumps of coal to appease the gluttonous appetites of our hungry izing glass-fronted stoves.

But in the end we had toughed it out and "weathered the storm." Just as had the Petersons and the Olivers and the Chaviers (and so many others across this land). And having been in the same boat, we shared a special comraderie.

But one thing for sure: we didn't want, ever, to be on *that* voyage again!

Ralph and I were also the survivors of another kind of big event. It was called "World War II and is often know as the largest, most devastating war of all time."

At this point in this chronicle, with your forbearance (and I'm sure that of Terry too) I will break into the little booklet "Memories for Teresa" that I had written for her a few years ago and use it verbatim to tell you a little about the early involvement of Ralph and myself during World War II.

It is called "The Day the World Turned Upside Down."

CHAPTER IB

The Day the World Turned Upside Down.[1*]

AS I now recall, it was a lazy grey Sunday afternoon. Typical of most Autumn days of this North country.

I was "taking it easy" upstairs in the little bedroom shared with my younger brother, Bill, leisurely listening to the Greenbay Packers "Game of the Week" on the other side of the big lake.

Sudden, all hell broke loose! A startling announcement filled the airways: (it was December 7, 1941) "Pearl Harbor had just been attacked. Our fleet had suffered grievous damage!"

We were called to arms! We were suddenly at war!

Never would our lives and those of our loved ones be the same again.

And, so like many, many others of our generation and other riled-up generations of the past, Ralph and I, his lifelong friend, joined up, said "good-bye" to our families and went off to war.

We had wanted to be with the Marines, but our "prowess" as athletes didn't count. We couldn't pass their peace-time oriented physical requirements (Ralph because of bent toes; me because of a sub-standard eye), so we settled for the Navy (and, in time, never regretted the "choice").

And therein lie two, self satisfying stories; one for each of us. They go something like this:

Ralph trained hard and learned well the techniques of the splint and the tourniquet and the use of pain-numbing needles; the wound-

---

closing sutures and the forceps and the scalpel, and the blood packs (and, oh yes: the body bags!) were soon second nature. And by now his services as a "top-notch," skilled medic were sorely needed and in great demand, particularly by the hard-fighting Marines, often the first to go in, and often the first to fall.

And when they called, Ralph eagerly answered: "Sure! Thought you'd never ask. When do we go!"

And go they did! An ocean ride later, he was there by their side, dodging bullets, tending to the wounded, soothing the dying in the snarly, vine ridden, Nippon-filled jungles... Always moving forward to one of our greatest victories on a far-off island (now legendary) called *Guadalcanal.*

My little story, though not so dramatic (and certainly not as heroic!) still gives me a certain ironic satisfaction when I think of it.

I has progressed quite well in the "E" divisions (electrical) and was eventually one of the three "senior" chiefs in charge of that division on the new battleship, *U.S.S. Wisconsin* (BB-64).

The "Wisky" was the flagship of the interception force. We had been in a number of engagements with the "enemy."

One was at an island called "Iwo Jima." It was there that I nearly "became" a marine (at least in heart).

While we were fighting off the "kamikazes" coming at us day and night, the Marines ashore were having a rough time of it trying to gain a foothold.

But the Japanese in their fortress positions weren't inclined to be easily taken. In fact, our forces ashore on the foot-burying, cinder slopes of that barren, shelter-less nightmare of a battleground were suffering severe losses and getting nowhere. And they asked the fleet for help ashore if at all possible.

These were our brothers in trouble! The word was passed for volunteers. The response was great. I was proud to be one of them, if our 120 man Marine contingent went ashore, I would be with them! So I checked out an old WWI Springfield rifle from the ship's armoury and waited.

But ashore I would never be. A Japanese fleet was sighted to the North and we sped off to intercept them.

By the way; I never once had the chance to load and become acquainted with that ancient Springfield rifle.

Perhaps that is why I am here today.

R.F.H. 2003

Going back for a while, to our Sunday dinner get together: the delicious meal continued to be a feast. And, in this company of joyous, happy revellers, an event to be long remembered And the coffee pot never ceased to make its rounds to make sure that no cup was ever empty.

And the little rooms of this little white house continued to ring with the laughter and banter (and once in a while, playful repartee) of friends forever.

And the usually quiet and reserved Teresa wasn't loathe to join in the fun. And once in a while, as the occasion presented itself, to mirthfully "set things straight."

And Ralph and I, lest by words we mar its beauty, were more than content to sit back in silence and enjoy the captivating charm of the wonderful scene playing out before us.

Perhaps a bit of un-admitted bashfulness may have played a part too.

That said, I think now would be a good time to say a little more about Terry. What a wonderful person she is and has always been!

CHAPTER IC

Teresa & Ralph & A Grand Reunion

JUST LIKE her mother and father and her sister Clarice and many others of the self-made patriotic "home forces" of the time, Terry did her part (and did it well) to assure that our country would eventually prevail, and the "boys would come home."

And like her brother Burt, who would soon follow her example, she took up drafting and worked in a number of places where her skills were needed.

It was a interesting sequence of events. I'll try to expound on these as best my limited knowledge of the details will allow:

It all began just after Terry graduated from Muskegon High School in June, 1943. The Borg-Warner Corp. was sponsoring drafting classes in the "Hackley Manual Training Building" in downtown Muskegon for the months of June and July. The classes would be held there six hours a day and the pay would be fifty cents an hour.

Terry eagerly accepted and the pay, she now tells me, was "big money" to her and her classmates in those long ago, end-of-the depression days.

Now a draftsman, Terry began her work in earnest: in the Aircraft Department of Continental Motors in downtown Muskegon. Her first assignment was very emotionally and patriotically rewarding: She would be one of the draftsmen (from sketches provided by engineering) of the engines for the first Army helicopter!

It was exciting! She was suddenly doing something really important that would help win the war!

Well, she was on that job for a year (until August 1944). Then the word came that the "love of her life," Ralph Vanderley, was on his way home from the Pacific and would be re-assigned as a medic to the Navy Supply Depot in Oakland, California and would be quartered, at least for a while, on the base. As soon as he arrived "stateside," he would be coming to see her as soon as he could. Also, he had a very important question to ask her! And Terry knew without a doubt what that question would be.

And she knew in her heart that her answer would be "Yes!"

And so, after buckets of calls back and forth across the nation, and tons of arrangements to keep things "on track," Ralph finally made it back to Muskegon, and they were married in a little church in nearby Grand Haven (August 19, 1944).

But the war was still far from over. It would continue for another year (until August, 15, 1945).

And "time and tide waits for no man" they say. This also applies to the Navy "leaves," and Ralph's was now nearly over. And the beautiful "honeymoon" that this happy, young couple had been enjoying so much had come to an end.

Time now to return to the world of reality. The U.S. Navy base at Oakland was beckoning. Time to pack up, say goodbye to the proud, teary-eyed loved ones who were there to see them off. Climb the steps of the waiting Greyhound bus; take their seats and head off to the West.

As soon as Ralph and terry arrived at Oakland, it was obvious that Ralph had been busy making arrangements: A cozy little apartment was waiting and would be their home, off-base, until the remainder of the war. And when I mention "their" home, I also mean the home of their baby, Bobby (proudly my namesake) who was born in an Oakland hospital just a few weeks before the arrival of some of the ships of the returning U.S. Fleet (including my battleship, *U.S.S.*

Wisconsin (BB-64)[2*] on the 15th of October, 1945.

And what a wonderful reunion we had!

Whether the water was too shallow by the docks at the bay side of the city, or all of the berths were too small or already taken, I don't really remember. In any event, we anchored a ships length or so offshore in "The Bay" and ship-to-shore motor launches quickly took over. And trip after trip, they were quickly filled with eager young sailors just back from the war on their first "liberty" anywhere in over a year.

One thing you could bet on: It would be a "hot time" in "Frisco" that night!

When it was my turn to take the brief ride and step down once again of "terra ferma," Ralph and Terry were right there and waiting. After hugs and smiles and grins all around, we beat a quick retreat, through the cheering crowd and honking horns, to their car that was parked nearby.

Then wedging ourselves onto the access lane, we sped across on the Oakland Bay Bridge and were soon in Oakland. A number of twists and turns later on a myriad of avenues and ways and drives, we suddenly swung off to a newly acquainted side street and there before us was the little multi-use building with their second story apartment.

Ralph parked the car in the driveway and picking up the things we would need for the night, we all climbed out, walked up the inside stair and knocked on the door to their apartment. And Terry called out, "Jane, we're back!"

The door quickly opened. Before us was their smiling, young baby-sitter. With a finger to her lips she cautioned, "Bobbie's asleep. Everything went well."

[2*] Should anyone be interested in further information on the *U.S.S. Wisconsin* (BB-64) and the participation in WWII, details can be found in my book *World War II Memories—U.S.S. Wisconsin*, BB-64, which I wrote and self-published (with the support of the U.S. Naval Institute) in 1987. It is all sold out now, but there are a few copies that I have retained for reference. Let me know. You may use them. —R.F.H.

Then thanking her for the good job she had done, Terry added, "Hope you can come back a little later. This is our day for a change. Tonight we are all going out on the town. It's been a long time since we were last together!"

Looking back now, we did have wonderful times. Not "riotous," or devil-may-care times as others may have had. But just simple, innocent, caring, glad-to-be-together times; out to a near-by restaurant for a steak, or a seafood dinner or the like (being together with those you respect and care a lot for, and who mirror your feelings, make such a big difference!).

On my last evening in Oakland[3**] we did a lot of reminiscing and conjecture on what the future might be like. First the Big Depression and the Big War. And with grit and determination—and a lot of luck—we had surprisingly survived them both. "Bring on the future, we'll take care of that too!"

And during the conversation I learned that Terry hadn't been just sitting on her hands waiting! As in Muskegon, she had been in the forefront of the battle here too—drafting the design of Navy tugboats and dive boats for a shipyard up the estuary in nearby Alameda.[4***]

For the next few pages on my brief sojourn with Ralph and Terry in the San Francisco Bay area, please indulge me as I borrow and reiterate some of the story from my book, "*A Sailor's Tales—WWII and India*" © 2006. Some of what I write may be repetition. Again—please

3** The *U.S.S. Wisconsin* (BB-64) would leave the next day for San Pedro, California. It was to be my last passage on that big ship; I had been one of its crew from the days of its final construction at the Philadelphia Navy Yard in 1943 until the end of the war (WWII) in 1945 (as a senior C.E.M.).

4*** This came as a real surprise to me. My first ship, the U.S.S. Motive (AM-102) had also been built in Alameda, California (by the General Engineering & Drydock Co). I was billeted in a nearby building (in Alameda) during its final construction and fitting-out in the Spring of 1943, and was one of the E.M.'s on her convoying in the Aleutian Islands area until the time we had retaken Kiska.

forgive!

Here goes!

From A Sailor's Tales—WWII & India

October 15, 1945

The Golden Gate is looming larger and larger up ahead. Our long "Going Home Pennant" has been streamed aloft with balloons; and a dirigible is circling overhead. It's music and voices sing out to welcome us home. What a wondrous greeting.

Then, under the crowd-lined bridge to anchorage. Home in the U.S.A. at last!

In the ensuing few days, many of your shipmates leave for home, at last, for discharge from the Navy. Their enlistments "for the duration," are now over.

The once crowded, happy, noisy ship no longer rings with their voices and the sounds of their rushing feet. It is silent like a tomb. It is filled with gladness mixed with sorrow: home at last! But many good shipmates and friends we shall never see again—and not much later, we too shall follow.

In the next few days I visit my high school best friend Ralph Vanderley and his wife Teresa (Terry) in their Oakland home.

Ralph is a PHM i/c presently doing duty at the Oakland Naval Supply Base. He has recently returned from combat duty as a medic with the Marines on Guadalcanal.

Terry (maiden name, Peterson) is a young sister of my wife Clarice. Their new son, "Bobbie," has been named after me. We have a wonderful time!

A few days later our revered Admiral Halsey slowly circles the *U.S.S. Wisconsin* in his gleaming white launch to say good bye and bid us all farewell. It is a sombre occasion. We are very moved, but we are now too few to line both rails, so we switch to the other side as his launch goes by and are proud in our hearts to have served.

October 29, 1945

U.S.S. Wisconsin weighs anchor and sails south from the "Golden Gate" to San Pedro. For many, including myself, this will be our last cruise aboard as crew.

October 31, 1945

U.S.S. Wisconsin slowly glides through the breakwater entrance and anchors offshore in San Pedro Bay. We are not alone—other ships of our diminishing fleet are all around us. But we are like fading ghosts of the past. It is eerily quiet, save for the ringing of identifying ship's bells in the foggy night to guide our small boats some.

For those who now leave forever, it is "Liberty and Leave" until the necessary paperwork is completed. As a child, during the "Great Depression," I and my family lived in the rolling foothills not far away.

I hire a taxi (for a now unbelievable five dollars) and visit the Smith's who still lived on Ridpath Drive. We have a grand time!

I go to their daughter's high school graduation. Next day I reciprocate and show Mrs. Smith around the *U.S.S. Wisconsin.*

But there is a sad note to it all! I phone the home of my grade school friend Johnny Ford and ask if, perhaps, he is home.

There was silence. Then a choked answer, "Johnny just died in a storm at Okinawa." A typhoon had swept the island soon after we had left and Johnny who had been waiting for a passage home, was swept away by the raging seas!

He was a wonderful friend of my childhood. I'll never forget our walks through the foothills and our meetings in our "fort" overlooking "our valley" in those days of (now) long, long ago.

How strange after all of those intervening years we had been no near—and yet so far.

November 28, 1945

Papers completed and now in hand, I leave the *U.S.S. Wisconsin* for the last time. Board a train to visit mother and Bill and Tom and sisters Marjory and Janie in Edgemont, Illinois. Then on the Great Lakes, Illinois for discharge.

January 9, 1946

Discharged from the U.S. Navy, I return home to sort things our. I am now a civilian and the future is strangely a wee bit scary.

End of Excerpt.

Going forward in time now, let's return to the story of that long-ago Sunday dinner at the Petersons (around 15 months after leaving the *U.S.S. Wisconsin*) and talk a little about the dear ones whose joyous, happy presence that day added so much to the wonderful fellowship, and whose caring, sharing ways throughout the years that followed have meant so very much to me and all others whose lives they have touched along the way.

CHAPTER ID

Amy "Sis" and Dean

AMY KARLEEN is the youngest of the six children of William (Bill) and Myrtle Peterson. The nickname, "Sis" by which she has always been known by her family, is not only an acknowledgment of kinship, but a proud assertion to all that this beautiful, lively, wonderful person is one of them. And an implicit warning to all who would even think of bringing harm to their little sister in any way: "Don't even think of it! You'll have to go through all of us first! And you'd be mighty sorry!"

And her brother Burt—closest to her in age and a constant companion and avowed protector—would be one of the first to be by her side and wade-in.

But charming and pretty as Sis was—and still is—she was no shrinking violet." Grit and determination were always in her makeup. She could hold her own. And like Tom Sawyer & Huck Finn, she loved the doing of adventure, and the satisfaction of finding things out by herself.

When I think back to old days when "Sis" first caught my attention, I am reminded of that lively, pretty little girl in denim, who was filled with the spirit of adventure and loved to explore and find out and do things on her own: Intriguing to me in particular was the time she set up a little tent in the front yard of her home on Burton Road and camped out all night in the company of her waggy-tailed, black and white dog, "Jacob."

And other times when she would come home smiling and invigorated from a day spent driving a "John Deere" (or perhaps a Farmall) tractor up and down the well-kept garden fields of their nearby neighbor, Bill Spears.

Long days ago now, for sure. But looking back at the good times sure brightens the day!

But the happiest—and the saddest—times were yet to come.

During her high school days at Muskegon High, Amy met and fell in love with her tall, handsome classmate, Dean Hodson. Kind, considerate, caring, attentive, always thinking of the other person first, they were an inseparable match. And sharing the same beliefs in God and the hereafter, they were "soul mates" in every sense of the word. And after Amy had graduated from High School, they were married in that same little white house on Burton Road.

But the Korean War, now nearing its end, was still raging. And Dean, who had graduated the year before, had recently joined up and was in his brand new army uniform beside her, and was proudly, solemnly holding her hand in his as they said their vows.

And I and my darling wife, Clarice, her smiling big sister, were at their wedding and were there to see them off.

A brief honeymoon later, and duty called. And Dean, now a member of the Army Security Forces, must answer.

This time though, it would not be just basics and practice. It was for the real thing. And it is off to Germany for God knows what in those long-ago unsettled years; and to the camaraderie and adventure of a lifetime.

And missing Dean terribly, and as adventurous as ever, Sis followed next year as soon as she could. What a wonderful, exciting three years they did have there together! Off-hour get-togethers with comrades from the base; evenings-out at the homes of welcoming families in the nearby towns and villages. Bus rides and train trips when on furlough to view the marvels of this captivating, beautiful, strange new land: Vineyard laden hillsides, castle-topped craigs overlooking the meandering, narrow roadways along the rock-walled drop-offs to the silvery threads of streams and rivers that silently, endlessly wound their way to somewhere far below. And not to be outdone; in the towns and cities there were the massive, beautiful Cathedrals and the little shops of the cuckoo clock makers busily at work on their raised tables and benches. And the inns and restaurants that would serve the most delicious meals—and would sometimes have a long, long "Alpenhorn" you could try to puff up your cheeks and blow on—if you had the courage that is—in front of all of those people.

And there were many other sights and things to do in those long ago days that only Sis, who was there at the time, could tell us.

But the most important event of all took place near the middle of their three-year stay in Germany: the birth of their first child, Pamela (Pam). What a welcome, beautiful little girl she was! And still is today as a wonderful, caring daughter with grown-up children of her own who lives nearby with her adoring, sentimental husband.

Time went by and Dean's deployment now over, they packed their gear and headed home. Their cozy little house on Francis St. in Muskegon was still waiting. And they opened the doors and walked in and stayed for a long, long time. And Dean went to work for the post office, and later Sis did too.

In time there were three more wonderful children—all happy, full-of-energy, inquisitive little boys: Charles, David and Rob. And they all went to church on Sundays where Dean was a Deacon and later an Elder.

But one day, when they were all through college and had good jobs and families of their own and it was time for Sis and Dean to sit back, take it easy and enjoy the fruits of the "good life" they so much deserved, a horrible thing happened! A large tumor was suddenly discovered next to Dean's brain! And their wonderful life and the future they had worked so hard for were now in real jeopardy. There was no time to waste. They had to move fast to see if there was anything that could be done. Fortune smiled on them! Their doctor had an answer: there just happened to be a state-of-the-art facility in Cambridge, Massachusetts—The Harvard Cyclotron Laboratory—whose specialty was devoted almost exclusively to the eradication of the tumors in oncology patients just like the one of Deans! In addition, the cost of these treatments, often for an hour or more each day (including preparation) and for as long as a month or more, would probably be covered by their medical insurance plans.

And to top off the good news, Amy (Sis) could stay at "Hope Lodge" in nearby Worcester, which was owned and sponsored by the Worcester Community Chest, until they were ready to return home.

Good news indeed! And almost before their good doctor had finished the telling, Sis and Dean were already, in their minds, on the way!

So, in the early days of February '94, they packed up their bags, boarded an airplane and winged their way East from the cold of winter in Michigan to the cold of winter in New England. But the cold didn't bother them a bit. The warm glow of promise in their hearts and their love for each other more than kept them warm!

Well, to "cut to the quick," the operation really worked! It was a shouting-out-loud, howling success! In fact, to Sis and Dean and the many who loved them it was a downright miracle—a prayer come true!

And the long hours spent on measuring and fitting and wearing the bronze hood with the proton beam guiding-hole in it. And the itchy minutes that seemed like days, lying still as a mouse under shielding blankets on the operating table while the busy little proton beam, under the guidance of skilled hands, probed and sliced at the tumor to do its job. All were tithes of patience and trust and badges of honor!

Eight wonderful years went by in the same little house on Francis Street. Then Dean became ill again and Sis nursed him and cared for him the best she could. But this time it was to no avail. On September 18, 2002, he was sorrowfully, sadly laid to rest in a nearby shady plot in Sunrise Gardens Memorial Cemetery.

Theirs was a beautiful marriage, sealed by everlasting love and understanding, and Dean's "death" on the milieu of this old earth is far from the ending. Not only is it now the time for beautiful thoughts and memories, Sis and Dean are together, even now, through their wonderful, constant communion in faith and prayer.

This, I and all others who have known them and loved them throughout the years, do firmly believe!

And in their times together, they did many wonderful things and shared many adventures.

The moral integrity of their four children and their commitment to be the best they could be attests not only to the wisdom of their parent's teachings, but also to the love for one another they shared.

As I now go on to write about my darling Clarice (we were married for fifty-six years), please forgive me if I have to pause a bit and wipe the tears from my eyes. She was such a beautiful, precious person! Even now, at church, I often have to get up and leave when my glasses fog up in the middle of a favorite hymn and I can't see the words; and she is no longer there to hold my hand and sing beside me.

There! Now I've said it! Time now to get on with this story[5*] and tell you a little more about Clarice, the love and pride of us all, who left us nearly a year ago; and is now smiling down, and waiting for us all in Heaven.

[5*] For the remainder of this little story about Clarice, I will rely heavily on excerpts from my long delayed book-in-process: *The Best of Times: The Worst of Times—Chances Are You're Next.* © 2006 R.F.H.

CHAPTER IE

Clarice

FOR MOST of her years prior to the early 1990's, Clarice was an active, energetic, full-of-life person. The world all about was a wondrous panorama of beautiful things to see. Intriguing mysteries to unveil, challenges to give a good try, and wonderful people to meet and befriend. And of friends, she had many along the way.

She had been in the best of health with no physical problems to be really concerned about prior to this time. Only the usual childhood afflictions of growing up: measles, mumps, chicken pox and the like that didn't pass her by! Bothersome, stay-at-home inconveniences more than anything else. And, as was the lot of most of us during those long-ago years, there were shots to take, pills to swallow, and vaccinations to endure in school—or by your family doctor if you had one—to ward off goiter (prior to the use of iodized salt) and lockjaw and later the dreaded polio.

And, as was the metamorphosis of the child through adolescence to adulthood, so were the changes in mind and spirit.

The direction and scope of these changes is greatly influenced by heredity. But the depth and impact on the well-being of our lives is much up to us through the environment of love and care and circumstance in which we live, and the horizons to which we aspire.

But we are fragile humans and we do wear out. Our challenge is to do our best. Our role is to pass on to others the best that was ours.

When Clarice was a child it was "hopscotch" and "jump-rope" and "jacks," and games of "tag" and "hide and seek," and sometimes cut-out dolls from the "funny papers," and other interesting, fun things that little girls would do.

For little boys it would be "mumbly peg" (with an open pocket knife) and marbles and hand-made rubber band "guns" of wood (with clothespin triggers and bullets sliced from old tire inner tubes) and "kick the can," and field hockey (with sticks sawed off from the bend of a tree limb).

Sometimes, if they were lucky enough to have a bat and ball among them there would be choose-up sides games of softball. The "diamond" was any old field.

Ah yes! Those were the wonderful days—for all who would dream. And of dreams, there were plenty.

Friendships were made—many for ever. And understandings of the world all about were in their beginnings.

And wondrous options and choices were excruciatingly oh so near! And available to all for the taking, or so it did seem.

The growing-up experience was wonderful: so much to see and understand and become a part of. So many interesting people to meet and have as friends. So many adventures awaiting. So many dreams to hopefully come true.

Time went on. Her grade school and high school and wonderful Hope College days now over—and graduate years at the Universities of Michigan and Washington too—Clarice went on into the field of teaching. Not the easiest life, for sure, but she loved it! It was more that a vocation: it was a way to be involved and pass on to others the lessons learned and the insights gained—and make a difference!

Many a night of those early years would be spent in the quiet of her room grading papers; adding notes of encouragement and preparing the next day's lesson plans.

And though she enjoyed walks through the park and treks downtown and visits with friends, on many another quiet, peaceful night she could often be found curled up on her bed with a favorite book, and through its enchanting, beguiling words of promise be carried off to lands of adventure and dreams.

And in time, many of those dreams did come true. And I came

along and we shared many dreams and adventures together.

Then, one day, as is the lot of us all, we were suddenly old. And sometimes not too well. And dreams disappeared, and nightmares and sorrow soon took their place.

And through the pain in her sweet, beautiful body, she was always smiling. And she tried so hard to get well, but it just wasn't enough. And late one night, the angels called and she is now in heaven.

Claire's death was the saddest, most difficult thing for me ever! She was the joy, the pride, the love of my life for nearly sixty years.

Never in all of those wonderful, glorious years we had together, was there reason for doubt or question of the other. We were keepers of the faith and holders of the light of humanity. And we loved each other so much!

When I was "down" or disheartened, she was always there to take my hand and give me courage. "Don't worry, Bob, there's always another day!"

And when she was failing, she tried so hard to keep going. And her tiny little breaths near the end, through her smiles, were so tragic.

And I often think of the time when Claire's "little sister," Amy, and our children, Anne and Don and Beth, were there by her side in her times of need. To us they were truly angels from heaven.

And now Claire is there and waiting. Often at night in the silence of our room and the now empty bed beside me, I still hear her sweet little voice calling.

And through the tears, I answer, "Yes, my darling Claire, God is with us—See you soon."

PART TWO

The Great Depression

INTRODUCTION

The Little White House on Burton Road

THE GREAT Depression wasn't "great" at all! Far from it! For all but the very most fortunate (and there weren't many of them) those were the worst time imaginable—ever!

Ask Claire's younger sister, Ardyce, who haltingly clutched at her big sister Claire's skirt one day and tearfully asked, "Why's mother crying?"

"Why, Ardy, we've lost our home. We couldn't pay the rent and she doesn't know where we can go or what to do."

Then think of their worried, dear father, Bill and the bevy of understanding friends and relatives who pitched right in, without being asked to help, and pooled the nickels and dimes and quarters they could find and bought a little lot; and dug a basement by hand; and moulded its concrete blocks in a home made wooden frame. And, after seemingly endless days and weeks and months of loving caring toil, ended up one day with a little white house so sturdy and straight that it still stands proudly today—more than sixty years later—well inside the city limits of Muskegon, Michigan on Burton Road, not far from the now seldom used railroad tracks that, in days gone by, once defined the outskirts of town!

CHAPTER IIA

A Smorgasbord of Problems & Questions

- Dad looses everything; there are many others in the same leaky boat
- In and out of a Pennsylvania Orphanage.
- Staggering, incalculable costs!
- Many how's? and why's?
- Intra-bank dilution of Demand Deposits.
- Irrational buying of stock "On the Margin."
- Monumental Pay-back burden of WWI
- Partisan Regulation of the economy vs. "Laissez Faire."
- Also, as mentioned in the following chapter: (The impetus) was the war; that unconscionable, life-taking, dream-breaking, shoot the works—forget about tomorrow war!

I can never look back to those horrible days of the "Great Depression" without feelings of pride and love—and almost reverence—for my mother, Marjory May, and father, Robert Sr. who worked so hard and caring for us, their children, to try to pull us through! But in the end, it was to no avail: Banks closes, one after another; no money, no jobs, no future. Hope died. There was nothingness, despaired ruled—you were on your own.

A little boy of five at the time, I was with my father that miserable day in '29 when he turned off the lights to his new "Deluxe Laundry" ("Largest West of the Mississippi River"), turned over the keys for his fifty brand new delivery trucks and sadly walked away. It was truly the end of a dream. Things would never again be the same.

From that day on, until Dad's death in a veterans hospital in Grand Rapids, Michigan thirteen years later, things never again were the same!

Oh, yes! Dad had tried real hard, and Mother—bless her dear heart and memory—persevered the best she could. Things were "tough," and sometimes seemingly even tougher.

My younger brother, Bill and I were even once in a Pennsylvania orphanage ("Bethesda," outside of Meadville I believe), until dear Aunt Jane Stansbury, Dad's oldest sister, and our equally dear Uncle Everet—a streetcar conductor on the "Cleveland Street Railway," suddenly found out one day (our day of "deliverance") and rushed right over and whisked us away (if that is what a 1924 Dodge could be said to do) and took us to their home in East Cleveland, Ohio.

From that day on, to two little, teary-eyed boys from a Pennsylvania orphanage, our dear Aunt Jane and Uncle Everet would be Jesus Christ and Mary for the rest of their lives, I kid you not!

I won't go into the details, but the rest of our family eventually found their way to Cleveland and the home of Aunt Jane and Uncle Everet to join Bill and myself. First, Mother and our little sisters, Marjory and Janie from Pennsylvania, after a brief sojourn at the home of Mother's own parents, Harry and Mae (Woodward) Line in Meadville, who were struggling themselves to survive.

Then later, our dear, nearly worn-out father from the "Okie"-hating, fast-degrading no man's land of California—a most difficult, heartbreaking trek for this gentle, mild-mannered man—an ordained minister (Presbyterian Seminary in Marysville College, Tennessee, I believe) of so much energy, so many dreams, and so much love for his family and concern for his fellow man. And was now all alone and just trying to get home.

How Dad finally made it—but only for a few more years—only God knows now.

One thing for sure though, whether by "riding the rails," "hitching," whatever rides he could get or just plain wearing out his shoes—

whatever the way, I know it was done with grace and concern for the fellow man that just happened to be beside him!

When Dad had finally returned and we were a family once again, the hard times had far from abated. And we moved all around the country to many places to find a way out and try to survive.

We were far from alone; there were many, many others. And we learned real fast just how terribly bad the times had become. And "to each his own" was a theme for survival, we weren't alone; we had company—lots of it! And we were in this storm-tossed, leaky boat together, and the same giant waves beset us. And to make it through to the haven of that distant shore that beckoned, each must pull an oar and all must bail together.

As we asked ourselves then and have continued to ask through the many years later—even today: Why? How in the world could such a tragic, horrible thing ever have happened?

We are not alone in the asking. Educators and scholars; office holders and office seekers; economists and bankers—and those who are just curious or like the challenge of a good mystery, still ask and seek the answer(s) today.

And there are many different answers and many conflicting theories. And they all can't be right! Or can they?

But through them all there seems to be a remarkable consistency. With our kind forbearance, lets now delve into the possibilities and the very relevant, influential backgrounds of the times under the five presidencies most immediately involved—Thomas Woodrow Wilson, Warren Gamaliel Harding, Calvin Coolidge, Herbert Clark Hoover and Franklin Delano Roosevelt.

The dilution of the demand[6*] deposit reserves, of the Federal Reserve Banking System was the final instigating problem that nailed

[6*] Economists later estimated that at least 90 percent of the dollar volume of monetary transactions in the United States are settled by means of checks drawn upon demand deposit accounts. (Ref. Pp 126, 127, *Money & Banking*, by Raymond P. Kent, 1951)

the coffin of the "good times" shut!

When sorely needed to meet the urgent (often frantic) withdrawal demands of quickly angered customers (particularly those who speculated on the market and bought stock "on the margin" with money in cash they didn't have but expected to get from their demand deposits in their banks) the counted-on bank reserves, in lawful money, weren't there at all. They were only row upon row of un-backed, unstable *promises* from one bank to another to another. And to the horror of their incredulous banker-investors, it was realized too late that, like teetering rows of dominos, those rows of unsupported promises—and the lawful money they were supposed to represent—could easily, quickly come crashing down and hurt them badly. And that is exactly what happened!

The appropriateness and interpretation of the "Gold Standard" was often questioned: Should the volume of grains of the gold per dollar always remain the same or should it be adjusted up or down ("managed") to increase or decrease the value of the dollar to "stabilize" the economy, consistent with the perceived need and the vagaries of supply and demand?

Should the President, through the actions of his Secretary of the Treasury, continue to have the authority to manage (increase) the quantity of currency in circulation to promote higher prices (and thus decreased inflation) by the issuance of gold certificates and by the reduction of the bullion content of the gold dollar?

Should the President of the United States, through his Secretary of the Treasury, also continue to have the veto power over the Board of Governors of the Federal Reserve System, to change the reserve requirements of member bank balances?

Should the concept of "laissez faire" be more our guide?

Minimum Controls; Minimum Government intrusion.

Managed by who? By what standard? For how long? What about state's rights? What about the role of the federal government?

What about the rights and obligations of us all in the divided responsibilities of federalism?

And, lest we be too hasty, it would be well to remember the trials and tribulations, successes and failures of prior administrations and the advice of others (perhaps not the most popular at this time) whom history has proven to be right.

Think of the lessons implicit in President Warren G. Harding's administration (1921-1923) on how to quelch an impending disaster.

When Harding took office in January, 1921, the Treaty of Versailles with its hotly debated proviso's and inuendos and divisions of responsibilities and demands for reparations was finally signed by all participants, and World War I had finally come to an end, the horrible impact of this gigantic struggle on the world, and its many peoples, was just beginning and would be there for a long, long time. As remarked by Paul Johnson in his outstanding book, "A History of the American People," (1997, pg. 642) "The Great War of 1914-18 was the primal tragedy of modern civilization, the main reason why the 20th century turned into such a disastrous epoch for mankind."

The cost of the "War to End All Wars" as it has sometimes been paradoxically called, was staggering! Finding a way to pay for it all, if a way could be found, was monumental!

And many who blindly clamoured for its "glory" and those who had benefited from its munificence, quickly distanced themselves from those who had to pay. And there were many of them; the accounting is there for all to see.

The financial costs of WWI to the federal government was ten times more than that of the U.S. Civil War and more than twice the combined costs of all U.S. Governmental operations (more than $112 billion) since its inception at the conclusion of the American Revolution in 1789!

The costs borne by the families and loved ones all over America was *incalculable*!

How can you measure the sadness of a loved one's leaving? Or the heartsick and sorrow of those left behind to wait and worry? And then do the jobs of two—and often the jobs of more—in their absence?

And what is the cost of terror and tears, when a telegram comes—and you are suddenly alone—forever?

And from the piney hills and hollers of the Appalachians, to the towering white peaks of the Rockies and through the wavy green grasslands of the prairies and the undulating, antelope-roaming gentle slopes of the hills and valleys in between, the youth—the wealth of America—heard the call and answered. To most the choice was easy: they loved their country and they were needed!

And, in time, many came back. And there was many a tale. But there were many others who never "made it" and would spend forever in fields like Flanders. And in many a lonely home there were broken hearts!

For this little treatise, I won't dwell too much on the involvement of the other contestants of World War I. I do think it appropriate and important, however, to have an understanding of the huge costs in lives and money of that horrible conflict, and how the subsequent actions undertaken by our government and the divisive interests that influenced those actions, precipitated and were the primary causes of the "Great Depression" that followed.

Just think! When we went to war against Germany (April 6, 1917) after the sinking of the British passenger liner, *S.S Lusitania*, the United States of America had a standing army of only 200,000 men. The other contestants had many millions more. A little more than two years later (June 28, 1919), by a massive effort involving many deaths of far-away fields of battle and huge amounts of money, our army had grown to approximately 4,000,000 men, half of whom (2,000,000 men) were overseas in the American Expeditionary Force (A.E.F.) led by General Pershing. The majority of those (approximately 1,500,000 men) had been in actual combat.

Proud to say: A number of the members of our extended family were right there in the middle of it all! We still think of them in honoured reverence!

- William (Will) Peterson, Minnesota (Croix de Guerre)
- Robert F.B. Hansbrough, Sr. (Bob), Kentucky
- Nellis Rhodes, Pennsylvania.

In retrospect: if the United States hadn't entered the war when it did, and if it had not played such a major role as it did, it is questionable that the "Allies" would have ever won!

Besides patriotic chagrin, the net result of it all, in the end, would be anyone's guess.

Getting back to the aftermath: Massive efforts required massive amounts of money! And in the doing, we spent plenty! And borrowed even more! And we and future generations (when it stops? Who knows?) were saddled with the staggering pay-back burden.

CHAPTER IIB

Thomas Woodrow Wilson

(Thomas) Woodrow Wilson, the 28th President of the United States (1913-1921) was born in the Shenandoah Valley city of Staunton[7*], Virginia on the 25th of December, 1856.

He was a man of "many contrasts" from the very start:

Seemingly unmotivated, uncaring, or just plain lazy at the time (as his upbraiding father had constantly reminded him), he didn't learn to read until the age of nine. The message suddenly sank in, and his languid ways left. And, as the larva suddenly emerges from its start cocoon to become a beautiful butterfly, the young Wilson emerged from his lethargy to become, not many years later, a son his father and his country and much of the world all around, could be proud of.

His quest for knowledge became a life-long obsession, not only for himself and his proud family, but for those all around who would benefit from its lessons:

Teacher, professor, college president, governor (New Jersey), President of the United States, world leader. He was a man of many "letters" and many credits—and many hopes and dreams. Many of those dreams would come to fruition. Others, sadly, would not.

I have exhaustively searched the records of the Wilson administration, and the stories and records on Wilson himself. Nowhere have

---

[7*] Many of the author's colonial ancestors—the Blairs, and Hansbroughs—were born and lived in Staunton, Virginia and the nearby Shenandoah Valley and Blue Ridge Mountain areas, more than two hundred years earlier. A number were members of nearby militia forces and fought in the French and Indian War and in the American Revolution. Ref. Exhibits #2A & 2B & *Land of Dreams, the Great Adventure.©*

I found evidence of any kind to my satisfaction to support the contention that Wilson "didn't try hard enough, didn't do enough," or "didn't know enough" to prevent the "Great Depression" or alleviate the destructive impact of its coming.

Exhibit III, at the end of this story, is a run-down of the major programs that were put into effect during Wilson's administration (1913-1921).

Few of these, if any I'm sure, had any significant negative impact on the economy of the times, or contributed to the onset, or eventual depth of the "Great Depression" that brought our country and most of the world "to its knees" a decade later.

Getting down to the basics: it wasn't just the economy of the time that was at fault, or just the laws of the time and their administrations that were to blame. *It was the war*! That unconscionable, lift-taking, dream-breaking, economy-shaking ("shoot the works; forget about tomorrow") war!

Before proceeding, it would be well to point out that the homily, "war is hell," also applies to its *aftermath*! And often, if not always, comes with a vengeance.

And, despite the best efforts of dedicated, well-meaning men, its inherent tragedy, in lives, destruction and disastrous social and economic consequences, can only be delayed or mollified—never stopped. What happened after World War I was no exception.

Who's to blame? How about us all! As inheritors of the bounty of this great, wonderful land of ours, shouldn't "we the people," who commit to govern, also share in its blemishes?

After the conclusion of World War I, the huge build-up of men, money and material that had been created to support the war was no longer needed; factories shut down, businesses closed their doors, and workers all over the land lost their jobs and their incomes with it.

And there was suddenly a mass exodus back to the small towns and farms from which they had come. But there wasn't enough money there to support the ways of life to which they had become accustomed. And they called on the government for help. But the government didn't have much money left either. So it raised taxes! (And sometimes they were pretty steep). And soon the tax-payers didn't have much money either. And then the payers became askers. And this "no-win" cycle continued—until Warren G. Harding became President (1921-1923). And when Harding "got wind of it," he cut government expenses real hard (40% they say) and stopped that old cycle "in its tracks." And things returned to normal again—until the last days of his successor, Calvin Coolidge.

CHAPTER IIC

Warren Gamaliel Harding

AMERICA IS fortunate to have had so many exceptional, well-liked, "man-of-the-people" presidents. Warren Gamaliel Harding was one of them.

Born into poverty on a small farm in Ohio, he rose from its sorrows and longings for a "better tomorrow" by hard work, determination and the trust and respect of honest, straight-forward, friendly people just like himself who were striving so hard to make their visions come true.

His "look-ahead, give it a try" attitude was contagious; not only to others, but to himself. "Success breeds success." It spurred him on.

With the help of several friends—and the $300.00 they had among them—he purchased the nearby town newspaper, "Marion Star,' and became its editor, then the director of several other small businesses.

From then on, as he steadily progressed up that hard to climb "ladder of success," his down-to-earth winning ways and his love for America and all of the wonderful things it stood for, didn't go unnoticed. Particularly by those in the political arena!

And he jumped into that arena with a will and went to work:

- Elected State Senator in Ohio (1898-1902).
- Lieutenant Governor of Ohio (1094-1906).
- Made the nominating speech for President-to-be William Howard Taft (1912).
- Elected President of the United States by a "landslide" (1921).

When Harding took office in January 1921, the United States and the world all around were in the midst of a serious "recession."

The restrictions and self-denials of the war years were over, and people spent and splurged in a frenzy as though there was no tomorrow. And prices rose again and again with the seemingly endless demands. But the "borrow from tomorrow" psyche of the war years was also over. This time you had to pay *now*! And the bad part of the "feast and famine" cycle began again. Wholesale prices in the U.S.A. had more than doubled—in the last five years—and multiples of that in Britain and Germany and other countries of the world.

Their money exhausted, people stopped buying. Factories slowed down or closed shop. Workers lost their jobs and then their savings. The old "good time—bad time, wheel of fortune cycle" was in action. It's pedal had to be speeded up fast to get it past "too late," and around to the part called "recovery"—and do it soon!

Then Harding and his Secretary of the Treasury, Andrew William Mellon—financier, philanthropist and statesman, an excellent choice for the job—put their heads together and roundly agreed: "If you can't fight trends that are normal (such as laissez-faire), join them and make them work *for you*." So that is what they did. And the economy now on the downside, they cut the expenditures of government too—by a whopping 40%. And to make sure that things would return to its "normalcy" (a favorite Harding term) and stay, Harding created the Bureau of Budget, under the Budget and Accounting Act (1921), with Charles Dawes as Director to monitor expenditure and make sure that never again "would everyone do as they damn well pleased!"

By the end of July—only seven months after Harding took office—the recession was over and the economy began to boom again!

In England,[8*] Prime Minister David Lloyd George improvised a system of piece meal controls and rationing. In addition, he added fiscal and monetary measures that restrained inflation "more effectively than in any other combat nation."

Further evidence that compliance with the precepts of "laissez-faire" really works to smooth out the rolling hills and valleys of economies left alone. But, when it comes to road washouts and rock slides along the way, bulldozers and bridges are sometimes needed (and someone must bring fuel for your idling car while you wait.)

Harding was an outstanding administrator with a conscience, always keeping the welfare of our country and its hard-working people in mind with three glaring exceptions. The members of his cabinet and the heads of major government departments were excellent choices too. Many went on to acclaim and fame in future years: Calvin Coolidge (Vice President), Charles Evans Hughes (Secretary of State), Andrew Mellon (Secretary of Treasury), Henry C. Wallace[9**] (Secretary of Agriculture); Herbert Hoover (Secretary of Commerce).

But the self-serving betrayals of three others—whose names I won't divulge (let their infamy live on in their own anonymity) were the hardest blows of all to the thunder-struck Harding.

He had trusted them as friends, but behind his back they had plotted and schemed for their own advantage with obviously few qualms.

One sold off huge stocks of governmental supplies, at prices far below worth, for a profit. (When confronted, he resigned!)

Another had furtively granted leases (for $400,000) of govern-

---

8 * Ref: *The Great Wave—The Price Revolution of the Twentieth Century* (pg 191) by David Hackett Fischer.

9 ** I was privileged to hear Henry Wallace speak about his "One-world" philosophy to a packed auditorium on the campus of the University of Michigan, Ann Arbor, when I was a student there in engineering in the Spring of 1946.—R.F.H.

ment oil reserves at Elk Hills, California and Salt Creek ("Teapot Dome"[10***]) in Wyoming. (He was jailed for a year!)

The last had secretly sold off governmental favors for a profit. (When confronted by Harding, he shot himself to death!)

According to William Allen White, editor and writer of the internationally known *Emporia Daily News* (Kansas), Harding had later told him, "I can take care of my enemies all right; but my friends, my God-damn friends, White, they're the ones who keep me walking the floors at night."

During the last days of July 1923, via a vigorous hat doffing, hand-waving stop over in Seattle, Harding collapsed for a while on a train while enroute to San Francisco. Once there, he was met by throngs of cheering crowds. But he wasn't "out of the woods," Harding's sojourn on this earth was nearing its end. Acknowledging the acclamations of the joyous crowd that was waiting, he walked unaided up the steps of the Palace Hotel then continued on to the room that was waiting, and fell down, head-first, on the bed where he died three days later (August 2nd, 1923)!

To the shock and disbelief of all who had known him, this warm-hearted, cigar smoking hero, who was on of them was now gone.

Like the last ride of Abraham Lincoln, not many years before, the long, sorrowful train ride home was one to be long remembered!

Silent crowds lined the tracks whenever there were people

Huge crowds stood in a dust storm in Cheyenne. The freight yards in Chicago were so packed with mourners for their last goodbye that the now-crawling train could barely get through.

Proof indeed that all of the money in the world can't buy greatness.

By the sweat of your brow, and kindness, it can only be earned!

---

10 *** Talk of the Teapot Dome "scandal" went on for years. I still remember the discussions when I was a little boy in a California grade school.

CHAPTER IID

Calvin Coolidge, "Silent Cal."

BEFORE GOING into the Depression-plagued years of Hoover, though, it would be well to take a break and say a few words about Calvin Coolidge, Warren Harding's Vice President, who succeeded him on August 2, 1923.

Unfortunate for the country as President Harding's death was, there could have been no better choice to replace him and represent the deep-down values and feelings of America than his own Vice President, Calvin Coolidge, who quickly arrived on the scene and took over. This I firmly believe! I am in good company and it is "high time" I feel that we the people of this wonderful land, begin to realize what an exceptional patriot and advocate for humanity we had in our 30th President, "Silent Cal!" From here on, in this little synopsis, I will just try my best to present some of the facts and some of the representative sayings of this remarkable man whose patriotism, I believe, could be likened to that of Thomas Paine, and whose advocacy for human rights, to that of Horace Greeley.

If you will, let's try to learn together:

Born in the small country town of Plymouth, Vermont on the 4th of July, 1872 (Independence Day), Coolidge's place of birth was a harbinger of his down-to-earth, small town leanings and the celebrated national holiday on which he "arrived" was an appropriate—but unintended—characterization of his obvious loyalty to his "founding father" ideals.

"Silent Cal," as he was often called, wasn't really all that silent—only when the occasion suited him and when he needed a shield to quiet the incessant babblers, discourage intruders, turn away hordes of uninvited office seekers, and keep unwanted advice-givers "at bay."

But to be honest, there were plenty of times when he just wanted peace and solitude for himself so he could do his job, and get on with his work. And there was always *plenty* of that!

Coolidge was truly a "man of the people" in word and deed. And his actions and pronouncement bear this out. He ardently stressed that the primary function of the government in a democracy is to "uphold the law" (the will of the people) and not to "tinker" (let the concepts of "laissez-faire" have its way). The ups and downs of the economy that will always happen in a free economy reflect the needs and desires of a free people in action. Oh, a little "tweak" here and there once in a while in its workings might help to keep things "on track." But, in general: "Hands off. Let loose the reins." A free country, if left alone, will almost always find the level most appropriate to its needs. Reckless interference in this "natural cycle" can do nothing but harm!

"It's not just the freedom to participate in the making of a law (and the definition of its borders) that counts, it's also the provisions that are made for its enforcement."

(as a corollary: without laws, there is no need for enforcement. And without enforcement, the law is meaningless—and anarchy reigns).

"We have too much legislation by clamor, by pressure. Representative government ceases when outside influences of any kind is substituted for the judgement of the representative."

It is worth noting that to minimize unwarranted interference in the creation and administration of the law during the length of his tenure, Coolidge never once had a press secretary!

CHAPTER IIE

Herbert Clark Hoover

HERBERT CLARK Hoover, our 31st President (1929-33), was born in the small eastern Iowa town of West Branch, August 10, 1874. His father, Jesse Clark Hoover, was a blacksmith. Both his father and his mother, Hulda Randall Minthorn Hoover, were devoted Quakers. The son, Herbert, carried on the theme of kindness and concern for the welfare of others. And throughout his life made every effort to "walk the walk." For sure things didn't always work out the way he and many other well-meaning men had hoped. But his efforts deserve plaudits of us all. History proves he tried read hard and did his very best.

And the vilifications that we sometimes hear about this well-intentioned leader are just plain unfair!

Orphaned when he was nine years old, he knew what it was like to be alone. And he vowed this should never happen to others if he could help it. But first he must prepare himself to be of service the best he could. Then working his way through high school and Stanford University (1891), he became a mining engineer and married his college sweetheart, Lou Henry, when he was twenty five years old. It seems they were a wonderful, happy match. Later, when he was President, "Lou" was known as a charming hostess to all who visited the White House.

Hoover's commitment to help his fellow man ran deep, long before he became President.

His expertise as a mining engineer and business man took him all over the world and he learned in his heart that, in many ways, we are really all brothers. And the fortune he accumulated in his work allowed him to pass on to others the bounty that was his.

His work as an organizer of relief operations during WWI really made a difference to those in dire peril. To those he helped and others who knew, it didn't go unnoticed! The admiring Russian novelist, Maxim Gorky, once wrote to him: "You have saved from death 3,500,000 children and 5,500,000 adults."

I totally agree with historian Paul Johnson[11*] that "the notion that Hoover was a hard, unfeeling man (later circulated by self serving "New Dealers") was entirely false!"

Lets learn a little more about the works of Hoover and I'm sure you will agree:

As Secretary of Commerce under President Harding (in addition to reorganizing and expanding the Department to more adequately reflect the needs), Hoover sponsored conferences to help the unemployed, initiated programs to conserve fisheries; and developed programs for public works.

As secretary under President Coolidge, Hoover sponsored research programs, actually engaged in promoting public policy on oil, conservation, Indian Affairs, public education, child health, housing, "social waste," and agriculture, wanted aid to flow to undeveloped countries and "deplored" the exclusion of Japanese for racial reasons from the 1924 immigration quotas.

When Herbert Hoover became President, he continued his efforts to help those in need and to try to get us out of the Great Depression, the background of which he had just inherited.

Unfortunately, though, history tells us that his efforts and intent were undeniably laudable. Hoover's philosophy and approach to solving the supply/demand problem was *on the wrong track*! And his corporate solution ways increased the depth of the depression and greatly extended the stay!

Instead of following the precepts of "laissez faire" and letting the

[11*] Author of *A History of the American People.* (p. 738).

ups and downs of the economy find its own level and balance out *as it almost always will in a free economy*, Hoover chose to micro-manage the economy from above in the hope that the benefits thus derived would pass on down to the consumers in the supply/demand chain, and hopefully all would benefit. And he insisted on keeping wages high and on drastically extending credit.

But he overlooked the reality that "demand" is more than the desire or the need to have; it is also intrinsically linked to *ability to pay.* And for the millions of workers who had lost their jobs and had no ability to pay or buy, this was no help to them at all! And those who could borrow went further into debt while others were destined to poverty and the streets.

Though Hoover's approach to the overall solution was on the "wrong track," he did try to help people; his "heart was in the right place."

During his presidency he did a number of other important things to try to ease the burdens of the ordinary "common man."[12*]

- Established the Reconstruction Financial Corp (RFC)
- Set up the Home Loan Bank
- Expanded the Farm Loan Bank.
- Supported legislation to relieve states and municipalities that were unable to bear the burden of the economic crisis.
- Increased government spending. Gave indirect relief to business and individuals via arrangements with the banks.
- "All in all" more public works were started in Hoover's four years in office than in all of the prior thirty! Among these were many that revealed his expertise and forward thinking as an engineer:
- San Francisco Bay Bridge.
- Los Angeles Aqueduct
- Hoover Dam (Later renamed "Boulder Dam" by his

[12*] Again, please refer to *A History of the American People* by Paul Johnson—an outstanding work!

depreciating successor, Franklin D. Roosevelt.)

- His attempts to join in the building of the St. Lawrence Seaway were defeated by Congress.

When Hoover first came into office, he cut taxes heavily. "Those of a family man with an income of $4,000 went down by two thirds."

But all of the programs he had initiated from the start of his presidency cost plenty of money. And Congress was suddenly "horrified" by the tremendous deficit and insisted that Hoover, who had lost its confidence in his running of the country, insisted that the budget be brought back into balance!

The 1932 Revenue Act saw the greatest taxation increase in U.S. peacetime history. The tax rate on high incomes jumped from 25 to 63 percent. From then on, until the advent of WWII, the economic status of the country was out of control. And Hoover, who had tried real hard to help the common man and bring things back to a semblance of "normal," became the target of the nation's ire.

The history of the world, it seems, is a repetitive sequence of "good times" and "bad times," each with much the same underlying causes.

And we forget, or don't want to remember the lessons. For we are only humans, replete with many emotions. And often these lessons and emotions are perceived to have different values, which are triggered by images of past experiences, expectations, desires for well-being and hope. And this has played out in history, and in our lives, in many ways. And the causes and effects of the "Great Depression" are appropriate examples.

We have already discussed the prior "little" depression under Harding, that when it was over—even into the time of Coolidge—it was time to get back on your feet; time to splurge, to buy brand new Fords or Pierce Arrows or even Marmons (Dad had one but soon "lost" it) or invest heavily in the stock market by buying shares "on the margin." With money you have to borrow—and *must* pay back *in cash, on demand*, when the market falls—and you don't have the money. And you suddenly realize that you have been too rash and have mortgaged your future and there is nothing left—and no way out!

And that is just what happened! Thursday, Oct. 24th, 1929: The value of shares plummeted "straight down" with no one buying. Speculators were sold out when they failed to respond to market pay-back calls.

Frantic crowds gathered on Broad Street outside the New York Stock Exchange. And nearly a dozen, well-known investors (it is alleged) "jumped out of windows and committed suicide!"

"Black Tuesday," Oct. 29th, 1929

Desperate speculators and investors began the first selling of sound stocks—for whatever they could get—to try to prevent ruin. To most, it was already too late.

Not only the U.S. but the whole world was suddenly plunged into the depths of a great depression.

Hoover tried real hard to get things back on track, but nothing really worked. What we really needed were giant doses of optimism and hope: not patched-up programs and promises. And, sadly, Hoover just wasn't able to get these going.

Suffice it to say: he lost the next election to a smiling man with just the needed charm and rosy outlook for the future—Franklin Delano Roosevelt—by a "landslide."

CHAPTER IIF

Franklin Delano Roosevelt

FRANKLIN DELANO Roosevelt, the 32nd President of the United States, was born January 30, 1882, to Sarah and James Roosevelt on the Roosevelt family estate, Hyde Park, six miles or so north of Poughkeepsie, New York, near the banks of the beautiful, busy Hudson River.

The lineage of both of his parents goes a long way back in American history.

Sarah's ancestry (family name Delano) traces back to the arrival of the "Mayflower" to America in 1620.

The forefathers of James Roosevelt trace back to the coming of Claes Martenszen Van Roosevelt from the Netherlands to "New Amsterdam" in the "new world"; also in the sixteen hundreds.

Claes, through the descendants of his son Nicholas, is the common ancestor of two presidents of the United States: Theodore (Teddy) Roosevelt (26th President), who lived at his "Sagamore Hill" estate at Oyster Bay, Long Island, New York, and Franklin Delano Roosevelt (32nd President) who lived at Hyde Park.

Eleanor Roosevelt (her maiden name was Roosevelt) was a fifth cousin of her husband "F.D.R." as well as a niece of his energetic, risk-taking idol: Theodore "Teddy" Roosevelt.

Franklin's father James spent lots of time with him—sledding, sailing and just having fun. And so did his doting mother, Sarah. He was her only child and the "apple of her eye."

When his parents were away, young Franklin was cared for by a number of governesses, often of different national backgrounds. From them he learned various languages including German and French.

All in all, his childhood was a happy, privileged existence. But he knew of no other. He didn't feel rich or poor. To him, it was just the normal way of being. And he enjoyed his childhood to its fullest with no misgivings. Sailing and bird hunting with a gun on his huge estate were wonderful adventures. Stamp collecting was fascinating: it told him of other times and other places. And being an avid reader, he was carried off in his mind to the world of the believable and unbelievable in far-away places. And often those visions would come true and he would visit many far away lands and peoples of the world for real. And in the process would gain insight of the ways and feelings of others that sometimes, by only being there and being a good listener, can be revealed.

In the fall of 1896, during the growing-up years when he was fourteen, Franklin began a more formal education: first at Groton School, then Harvard.

His introduction to Rector Endicott Peabody at Groton had a big influence on his life leading him to an understanding that Christian values are not exemplifies by words alone, but by action to put the precepts into practice.

After Groton School, Franklin went on to Harvard (and later Columbia Law School) and while he was there he met and fell deeply in love with Eleanor Roosevelt, the daughter of his Godfather Elliott and the niece of Theodore Roosevelt. A year later (in 1903) they were engaged. Two years after that, when Eleanor was nineteen years old, they were married in New York City on St. Patrick's Day.

It was a wonderful match of two starry-eyed young people of high moral and religious ideals who, throughout their lives, wanted so much to be of help to unfortunate others of this world.

Through Eleanor's ever caring ways and guidance—and remembering the teachings of Rector Endicott Peabody of Groton School too—Franklin learned of the plight of others far less fortunate and are far less endowed. And was reminded that, beneath our facades of seeming unconcern and indifference, we are really much the same.

And that, for those 'without," how little help and encouragement it takes to make such a big difference.

And in his heart, he vowed that this should not be. And he committed to fill-in the chasms of unconcern and indifference that separates us all. And, in their places, build roads of communication and understanding where all can travel to the extent of their abilities to an enjoyable, fulfilling, meaningful better life.

And being close to his much-admired, exciting "Uncle Ted"—Theodore Roosevelt, 26th President of the United States—didn't hurt the soon to arise "F.D.R." one bit.

And he was imbued with the challenge to forget about the tangles of convention when you know you are right—particularly when it comes to the so-called "game of politics.' And don't be afraid to jump into the arena with the lions and tigers and best them at their own game!

And if those lions and tigers just happen to be in the form of foreign threats, powerful monopolies, and exploiters of the poor and down-trodden—well *so be it*!

Another thing too: when it comes to the mechanics of fairness, social justice and the well-being of an economy that fosters or allows these bad things to happen, the precepts of "laissez-faire" were seemingly always in mind; the economy is like a delicate heirloom, watch. Don't tinker with its setting or wind it too tight. It could easily break—particularly if you don't know what to do.

Franklin Delano Roosevelt: "Man of the People." For sure—and I am far from alone in the believing.

Let's delve a bit now into some of those "arenas" where he fought the good fight and did his best.

History now tells us that he wasn't always right and things didn't always work out But it wasn't, for sure, for not trying.

In 1941 when he was the President and in his third term of office, F.D.R. remarked to an assembled group of teachers that "there was no such a thing as a proven system of economics. I took economic courses in college for four years and everything that I was taught was wrong. The economics of the beginning of this country are completely out of date. We haven't yet learned from experience. We are still groping."[13*] Obviously we all have much, yet, to learn.

Perhaps I am "gilding the lily," but I don't think so! I and many others of my "soon-to-be-at-war" generation were there during the years of the "Great Depression" at some of its worst and though not truly understanding the background and implications of what was going on then, time has revealed how very fortunate we were—as were the generations of this great nation that followed - to have had such a well meaning advocate and fighter for justice and fairness and brotherly understanding who was almost universally known by the simple, meaningful description: "F.D.R."

After passing his New York State bar exam during his last year at Columbia Law School, Franklin, now an attorney, took, an entry level job as a law clerk at a Wall Street firm of corporate lawyers. It wasn't a very prestigious poison, but dealing with small claims cases and learning about the down-to-earth daily problems and challenges of the very poor and their desperate efforts to overcome them was a real education in itself. And one that would play a big part in his thinking and judgements of relative values for the rest of his life.

With this in mind and coupled with the urgings of his idol, "Uncle Ted," he decided to put all of this legal dilly-dallying behind him and go into public service. His rise after that was meteoric! Never, ever would he regret this life-changing decision. And standing proudly beside him was his dear wife Eleanor. She would be with him all of the way.

And just as had Warren Gamaliel Harding and others before him, he jumped into that arena with a will and went to work:

- Elected Senator of New York (1911-1912).

[13*] Ref. *Franklin D. Roosevelt—A Rendezvous with Destiny* by Frank Reidel, page 17.

- Assistant Secretary of the Navy under President Wilson (1913-1920).
- Stricken with polio (1921). A bad disheartening time. I'll go into that a little bit later.
- Presented name of Alfred E. Smith to the Democratic Presidential Convention (1924).
- Elected Governor of New York State (1928-32).
- Took office as President of the United States replacing Hoover (1933).

Earlier as the presidential years of Woodrow Wilson were coming to a close by the end of 1920, it was obvious to all but himself in the Democratic Party that it would be best to pass-on the baton of power to others more likely to be able to carry on, and hopefully win, in the developing presidential race. And it shouldn't be someone who would continue to stress that we join the League of Nations. The tragedy and distress of the recent World War (WWI) had left its imprint on the feeling of this country for sure. The people had their fill of squabbling with the rest of the world. They just wanted to get on with their lives in peace and by themselves for a change. The party and its candidates who offered this would get their vote.

And that is pretty much the way the presidential election of 1920 turned out:

For the Democratic "slate" it was James M. Cox, governor of Ohio for president, his running mate for vice president was Franklin Delano Roosevelt, assistant secretary of the Navy in Wilson's cabinet.

For the Republicans it was Warren G. Harding, senator from Ohio for president and Calvin Coolidge, governor of Massachusetts, for vice president.

The candidates on both sides were excellent, well-meaning men; dedicated to the doing of what they could for our country. But the much disturbing spectre of the recent war years shouldn't be dismissed and Harding's countering theme: "Let's get back to normalcy," played a big part. And it should be no surprise that the Republican Party under Harding & Coolidge won handily!

But in the process, though he had been on the losing side, the charming, winning ways of Roosevelt was making itself felt. And his star of ascendancy, in the public eye, bas beginning to shine a little brighter. And his resolve for the future was strengthened: "You don't go into a battle for second place; you go in to win!"

And this was played out in future campaigns and in his four coming presidencies. Even when his rise to the top was slowed and made much more difficult by a lingering, sudden attack of the dreaded polio. But "lingering" is a mild word to describe its terrible impact: for the rest of his life he could never again walk or dress himself unaided. Or ride around in a car, or go out sailing—that he loved to do—or stand at a podium to make an address before a soon admiring crowd without the help of others.

It was a sobering, often heart-breaking, down-to-earth experience. And a wake-up call (if you will): In spite of his numerous advantages of wealth and care and adventure and education and extolled family lineage, he really at heart wasn't much different from the millions of unextolled, others with unheralded backgrounds and little or no wealth who packed the halls and aisles of employment agencies looking for work, and lined the streets hoping for hand-outs and went to sleep tired and dejected and hungry in the cold, cold nights.

And sensing the problems and discouragement they faced, he vowed there must be a solution. And come "hell or high water," he would fight for those untold numbers of nameless others, who had souls and dreams just like his own, and find a way out.

And history tells us, that is just what our hard-working, dauntless, never-give-up President known as "F.D.R." did. And many years later, to this day, we and the generations that follow, are the fortunate beneficiaries.

The Democratic National Convention of 1932 convened in Chicago, Illinois with feelings of great hope and expectations that they could turn the horrible economic and social conditions of the time around.

They had a "platform" that boldly reflected the needs and desires of the people, and among them they knew they had the right man, at the right time, to push-through their simple, yet many-faceted optimistic rescue program for national recovery.

The plans and strong feelings of that man were already mirrored in their "platform."

Franklin Delano Roosevelt, the hard-fighting never-give-up Governor of New York was overwhelmingly their choice for President; and to augment the "ticket"—and fight by his side they hoped—would be John Nance Garner, Senator from Texas and Speaker of the House of Representatives.

But Garner, although liked by Roosevelt, and strongly for "the people" too, wasn't always inclined to go along with F.D.R.'s "too authoritive approach" and was often more in favor of stronger consensus with the Congress and its constitutionally defined legislative powers and prerogatives.

[14*]The Democratic Party Platform of June 30, 1032 declared that "the causes of the unprecedented economic and social distress we were in, were the disastrous policies, pursued by our government since WWI, of economic isolation; the fostering of mergers of competitive businesses into monopolies; the encouragement of indefensible expansion and contraction of credit for private profit at the expense of the public!

They committed to, and advocated, that the following remedial actions be undertaken as soon as possible, to begin recovery.

- Immediate and drastic reduction of government expenditures by abolishing useless commissions and offices.
- The consolidation of departments and bureaus and the elimination of extravagance to accomplish a savings of no less than 25% in the cost of federal governments.
- A balanced budget based on revenues raised by taxation and on ability to pay.

[14*] Ref. *Documents of American History* by Commager, p. 417-419.

- An international conference to consider the "rehabilitation of silver."
- Competitive tariff with reciprocal agreements with other nations to restore international trade and facilities of exchange.
- Extend federal credit to the state to provide unemployment relief.
- Expand federal programs such as flood control and waterways.
- Reduction of labor hours.
- Unemployment and old age pensions under state laws.
- Restore agriculture.
- Better financing of farm mortgages.
- Preferential credits for the redemption of farms and houses sold under foreclosure.
- Extend the development of farm coops.
- Control crop surpluses.
- Retain a Navy and Army for defence but weed out unnecessary costs.
- Strengthen and enforce anti-trust laws to prevent monopolies and unfair trade practices.
- Expand the conservation, development and use of the nation's waterpower "in the public interest."
- Protect the investing public by requiring the revelation of info on bonuses, commissions, principal invested and the interest of the seller.
- Regulation of holding companies which sell securities in interstate commerce; rates of utility companies operating across state lines; exchanges in securities and commodities.
- A more rigid supervision of national banks and prevent the use of their money in speculation.
- "Full measure of justice and generosity" for all war veterans who have suffered disability or disease caused by, or resulting from actual service in time of war and for their dependents.
- Settlement of international dispute by arbitration.

- No interference in the affairs of other nations.
- Adherence to the World Court with reservation.
- International agreement for arms reduction.
- Cooperation with nations of the Western Hemisphere to maintain the Monroe Doctrines.
- Oppose cancellation of foreign war debts.
- Independence for the Philippines; ultimate statehood for Puerto Rico.
- Employment of American citizens in the operation of the Panama Canal.
- Simplification of legal procedure and reorganization of the judicial system to make the attainment of justice speedy, certain, and at less cost.
- Continuous publicity of political contributions and expenditures.
- Strengthen the Corrupt Practices Act. Enforce severe penalties for misappropriation of campaign funds.
- Repeal the 18th Amendment (Prohibition of Intoxicating Liquors).
- Condemn paid lobbies of special interests to influence members of Congress and other public servants by personal contact.
- "We condemn the Hawley-Smoot Tariff Law, the prohibited rates of which have resulted in retaliatory actions by more than forty countries, created international economic hostilities, destroyed international trade, driven our factories into foreign countries, robbing the American farmer of his foreign markets and increased the cost of production."

"Equal rights to all; Special privileges to none."

A very ambitious program for sure. But this "shot in the arm" was just what the country needed! And the newly elected president, Franklin Delano Roosevelt, eagerly took up the challenge and jumped into the arena with the lions to do it all—and more![15*]

From here on, in this story, "its all history." And yes, that is what I am writing about. But "too much paint on the canvas hides the picture." What I would like to do now is present a "score sheet" (if you will) of the players involved, the way things turned out, and the feelings and emotions of the times in the "doing."

The "Platform" of the Democratic Party at the convention in 1932 pretty much outlines the scope of its plan to overcome the Depression.

The Inaugural Address of President Roosevelt, March 4, 1933, details his commitment to fight the enemy (often ourselves) that held us (and better times) back (Re. Exhibit IV).

In the process I may present a little of, what I feel, is interesting background history.

And in the doing, I would like to point out that this part of the story is primarily about the "Great Depression" and not of the later events of WWII and the ups and downs of the economy that unalterably, predictably followed.

I'll try to be brief.

On March 9, 1933, only five days after the beginning of Roosevelt's first presidency, Congress went into an emergency, special session that continued, under the guidance and prodding's of our also hard-working new President, for the now legendary, next Hundred Days.

It can be said with much assurance, that "more decisive legislation" was enacted by Congress during those days than in any other Congressional session in history!

Programs and Proposals Initiated by or Carried Over From Prior Presidental Administrations:

Jan 22, 1932 (Act of Congress)

15* Please refer to Exhibit IV: Roosevelt's first inaugural address, March 4, 1933.

- Reconstruction Finance Corp. (R.F.C.)
- Provided a billion dollars of capital to 6,000 banks to insure the success of the Federal Deposit Insurance Corp. (F.D.I.C.)
- July 22, 1932 (Hoover)
- Federal Home Loan Act—Divided the U.S. into 12 districts with a home loan bank in each.
- Designed as a re-discount institution in the field of real estate finance with functions similar to those of the Federal Reserve Banks in the field of commercial banking.

Programs and Proposals Promoted by "F.D.R." & Congress During F.D.R.'s First Administration (1933-37).

March 6, 1933

- Emergency Banking Act of 1923
- Authorized National Banks, upon approval of the Comptroller of Currency, and of the owners of the majority of their outstanding stock to issue non-assessable preferred stock which could then be sold as a new source of capital, to the general public or to the Reconstruction Finance Crop. (R.F.C.).

April 20, 1933

- Executive order by F.D.R. to abandon the gold standard.

May 12, 1933

- Agricultural Adjustment Act (A.A.A.)
- The most important of several acts to give relief to farmers:
- To raise prices of agricultural commodities to that of pre WWI levels, through voluntary crop reduction.
- Also authorized the devaluation of the gold dollars by not more

than 50%.

May 18, 1933

- Tennessee Valley Act (T.V.A.)
- Undertook a broad program of economic and social reconstruction of the Tennessee Valley Regions.
- Construction of dams, transmission lines, electrification, withdrawal of marginal lands, re-forestation, promotion of public health, etc. via a corporation for the operation of government properties near the rapid-running waters of the Muscle Shoals area of the Tennessee River in Alabama.

June 16, 1933

- National Recovery Act (N.R.A.)
- Was ruled unconstitutional by the U.S. Supreme Court via the decision of the "Schecter Poultry Corp. vs. United States" case, in 1935, for two basic reasons:
- Improper delegation of legislative powers to the President.
- Unconstitutional regulation of interstate commerce and was accordingly terminated by F.D.R. on Jan 1, 1936.

June 16, 1933

- National Industrial Recovery act (N.I.R.A.)
- Approved by Congress on the last day of its 100 day emergency session.
- Was, in some respects, the "most extraordinary law passed by an American Congress!"
- Provided for federal control of the entire industrial structure of the U.S.
- Title I: "Industrial Recovery"—Removal of obstructions to the flow of interstate and foreign commerce.
- Title II: Public Works and Construction Projects.
- Note: By 1933, a deflationary movement had been underway for over two years. The number of unemployed had soared to a total of 13 million; wage rates continued to be cut. In an

effort to turn things around this act was passed to start the comeback of industry.

- It was, in effect, a companion to the Agricultural Adjustment Act (A.A.A.) which strove to help farmers.

June 16, 1933

- Farm Credit Act of June 16, 1933
- Encouraged the creation and expansion of co-operated associations and provided for special banking facilities to supply them with both fixed and working capital.

June 16, 1933

- Emergency Railroad Transportation Act
- Provided for the reorganization of the railroads via mergers & consolidation of terminals, etc.

July 13, 1933

- Home Owners Loan Act
- Designed to assist distressed home-owners in the refinance of defaulted, or about-to-be defaulted mortgages on more favourable terms.

July 17, 1933

- Cotton Textile Code
- Established minimum wages for cotton workers:
- For Southern Section $12.00/week for 40 hrs. work
- For Northern Section $13.00/week for 40 hrs. work.

Winter of 1933/34

- Civil Works Administration Act (C.W.A.)

A temporary emergency program initiated by the deep concerns of President Roosevelt and the urgings of his trusted, former social worker friend, Harry Hopkins to do all they could as soon as possible to help the millions of desperately needy others of this country who had no other place to turn to carry them through the winter.

And, sensing the urgency of the human tragedy unfolding before them, both went to work with a vengeance to try to save their people. And with no time to wait for Congress and legislation, they garnered the needed funds from existing programs and gave millions of laborers and artists and teachers work in whatever could be found or devised to do. And, throughout the land for many years later, roads and bridges and art work in post offices and federal buildings still bore the imprint of their labors.

And in the process, the economy of those long ago days was enriched by millions of dollars. And the lives of untold numbers of fellow Americans were saved.

And for Franklin Delano Roosevelt, Harry Hopkins, and all of their selfless, hard working fellow workers who made this all possible, I'm sure we can all agree that this, indeed, was one of their "finest hours!"

November 16, 1933

- Recognition of Soviet Russia by executive decision (F.D.R.) for economic reasons.

March 24, 1934

- Recognition of the Philippines to offset the looming potential threat from Japan that had began to flex its muscles in nearby areas of the Far East.

July 5, 1935

- National Labor Relations Act (NLRA) ["Wagner Act"]
- Passed by Congress to replace the invalidated National Recovery Act (NRA). (In reality an extension of the Norris La Guardia Act of Hoover's administration, March 20, 1932).
- Extended many advantages to labor: the right to organize; the right to partake in collective bargaining and restore the equality of bargaining power between employers and employees.
- Excluded from this act, however, were individuals employed

as an agricultural laborer, or in the service of any family or person at his home, or any individual employed by his parents or spouse. The National Labor Relations Board, however, was constantly taken to task by rival A.F.l. & C.I.O. labor unions who charged discrimination by the Board in favor of one or the other of those labor organizations.

August 14, 1935

- The Social Security Act
- Although legislation began as early as 1929, it was not until the depression had run its course for six years, that the Federal Government took action on this subject: An act to provide for the general welfare by establishing a system of Federal old age benefits, and by enabling the several States to more adequately provide for aged persons, blind persons, dependent and crippled children, maternal and child welfare, public health, and the administration of unemployment laws; to establish a Social Security Board to raise revenue "and for other social purposes."

Note: I can honestly say with all of my being, "Thank God for Roosevelt and all of his hard working, good-minded followers and associates who had the courage and tenacity to keep after this most crucial fundamental need and push it through!

Let me tell you a very personal story of how much its "Title IV, Aid to Dependant Children" made such a difference!

After our family of seven had moved to Traverse City, Michigan from Kentucky in 1939 (more about that in the following chapter), my dear, worn-out father became desperately ill and spent the next three years trying to recover in the Veterans Hospital in Grand Rapids. And my dear little mother and we, her five children were suddenly all on our own with no income, no savings, no money.

Being "scared" doesn't nearly describe our feelings of despair! We were numbed almost beyond emotions.

But others had been watching, and they stepped right in to help.

And the grant of sixty-four dollars a month from "Aid to Dependent Children," and the locally-generated funds and help from the Grand Traverse Welfare Department—under the guidance of Bertha Miller Soderburg mother of my classmate Mary)—was like "manna from heaven" and pulled us through.

That was a long time ago, I know, and a lot of water has "passed under the bridge," but I and my family shall be forever grateful and, in the names of those still with us and in the memory of those now gone, let me now express in words what we have always felt in our hearts: "Thank you Traverse City and thank you President Roosevelt. We shall never, ever forget!"

Programs and Proposals Promoted by F.D.R. & Congress During F.D.R.'s Second Administration (1937 to 1941)

Major Elements of the Democratic Party Platform—June 25, 1936 (At Convention held in Cleveland, Ohio)

- Continue to promote plans for rural electrification.
- Vigorously enforce existing anti-trust laws.
- Reduce cost of Government.
- Continue to fight to lower the tariff barriers of other countries against our exports of agricultural and industrial products.
- Continue to improve soil conservation and domestic agricultural allotment programs with payments to farmers.
- Pledge the full cooperation of the government in the refinancing of farm indebtedness at the lowest possible interest rates over a lengthy time of years.
- Pledge the immediate extension of the monetary system

through the classified Civil Service.

January 1937

Franklin Delano Roosevelt (with Vice President-to-be John Nance Garner, Senator from Texas) soundly defeats Republican candidate, Alfred M. Landon, governor of Texas and running mate Colonel Frank Knox, by a "landslide" win of 523 electoral votes to 8 and takes office for the second time.

May 1 1937

- The Neutrality Act of 1937
- Enacted by a joint resolution of Congress in response to the outbreak of war between Italy and Ethiopia in May 1935, and later, by the Civil War in Spain. This important Act gave broad powers to the President to "prevent the export of arms, ammunition, or implements of war from any place in the United States to any belligerent state (named in his proclamation) or to any neutral state for trans-shipment to, or for the use of any such belligerent state…"

Also prohibited and/or controlled by this Act during the times of foreign wars when the U.S. was "neutral," were the following actions:

- Prevent the transport by domestic or foreign ships: fuel, men, arms, ammunition, or implements of war or other supplies, to any warship, tender or supply ship of a belligerent state.
- Prevent the use of territorial waters of the United States by the submarines or armed merchant vessels of a foreign state.
- Prevent American vessels engaged in commerce with any belligerent state, or any belligerent state wherein civil strife exists, to be armed or carry any armament, ammunition or implements of war, except small arms and ammunition for small arms "which the President may deem necessary."

1937

Reform of the Federal Judiciary—Inferior Federal Courts, and the United States Supreme Court.

For many other administrations prior to that of Franklin D. Roosevelt; there had been deep feelings of displeasure about the seemingly arrogance of the Supreme Court and his unwillingness to hear or take into consideration the "will of the people" that had been repeatedly expressed and made known to them by their representatives in many times and in many lawful ways.

The most important tenet of any representative form of government lies in the doctrine that they who are elected to office—by the people—are there for but one basic reason: to mirror the moral needs and desires of those who have elected them to office. And to do so in the most appropriate, moral and legal ways to assure, to the extent possible, that those needs and desires can be effected in a manner consistent with the desires and needs of others in the larger community in whose sphere of influence they live.

A number of Roosevelt's important "New Deal" economic and financial reform projects intended to bail out the failed economy and bring relief to the desperately needy poor, were thwarted by the Supreme Court which held that their derivation by the President and his Executive Dep't was based on the arbitrary assumption of legislative (and quasi-judicial) powers, not given to them by the U.S. Constitution.

On the other hand, President Roosevelt felt strongly that the Supreme Court, *itself*, had often over-stepped its constitutionally-defined bounds by its frequent assumptions (at least in effect) of both legislative and executive roles which were, also, not given to it by the U.S. Constitution.

An impasse of conflicting roles and philosophies for sure. But there was only one Supreme Court, one Congress, and one President. Who was there left to legally make the decision? Go directly to the people? Consensus of state legislatures? Compromise? What else?

Bu there was another approach that just might work. And its basis was in the Constitution:

Article III, Section #1 of the U.S. Constitution states: "The judicial power of the United States shall be vested in one Supreme Court and in such inferior courts as the Congress may, from time to time, ordain and establish. The judges, both of the Supreme and inferior courts shall hold their office during good behavior, and shall, at times, receive for their services, a compensation which shall not diminish during their continuance in office."

It was obvious that the tenor of the justices, both of the U.S. Supreme Court and the inferior court, was subject to the purvey of Congress.

More importantly no mandatory *retirement age* for those justices was mentioned or even inferred, in the wording of the Constitution!

Therein, Roosevelt felt, lay the basis for the solution of the impasse with the courts!

A number of the justices of the Supreme Court and the inferior courts too, had planned to stay on for life. Others for a long, long time until they just felt like leaving. Being a judge was exhilarating; the esteem was exhaulting; and the monetary remuneration didn't hurt one bit either! But what if this all was threatened—*by a cap on maximum age.*

And that is just what F.D.R. decided to try. Maybe now the courts would begin to think a little more about the welfare of the people and a whole lot less on the manipulation of arbitrary words to get their own special interests and private feelings across.

Well the word got around fast! And there was an uproar throughout the length and breadth of the land! And though Roosevelt lost the fight—so to speak—he won in the end the battle. Never again would his fights for the welfare of the poor, the aged, the children, the destitute of this country who couldn't speak for themselves be unfeelingly cast aside in the cauldron of reckless abandon by those who were supposed to protect them.

After the disastrous "bank crash" of 1929, employment had continued on a downward spiral, with little let-up, until the encouraging "shot-in-the-arm" election of our cheery new down-to-earth President,

Franklin Delano Roosevelt in 1933.

And, even though our economy had gradually improved during his next two terms of office, our nation was still deep in the throes of the Great Depression and hurting: Millions of people were still out of work and many others were on borderline incomes.

Statistics reveal that nearly a quarter to one third of all families in America had no income at all during those devastating years.

Callous and indifferent to the horrible, almost unthinkable human consequences of war as it may sound (and, believe me, in no way do I endorse it, as a means for economic, or well-being ends) but the facts and statistics cannot be denied:

Not until our fleet at Pearl Harbor was attacked by Japan on December 7, 1941 did we, as a nation, really begin to see the awakening light that had lain unattended in our minds for years.

Not until then, did we the inheritors of this wonderful land of ours with all of its beautiful people and fine traditions, begin to realize that all around were others just like ourselves with the same hopes, the same fears, the same feelings. And that if we were ever going to beat back the intruders that beset us, whether they were in the form of other nations, the economy, or other undesirable things the future may bring, we couldn't win alone. We had to do it together.

And if we didn't have the means at the time to buy the clubs and axes that would be needed for the fight, then we must borrow from the future. For if the future should never come because of our inaction, then what we had lain away would never again be of value or be seen.

November 14, 1939

The Neutrality Act of 1939, ("Cash and Carry Act")

The outbreak of the Second World War, the month before in September, had a modifying effect on the intensity of the opposition of many of the Senators who were sympathetic to the plight of England who was now struggling valiantly in the fight of her life for survival. Although this Act was similar to the Neutrality Act of 1937, they went along with its acceptance...but there was one important "Cash and

Carry" qualification:

"Belligerents may purchase and remove war munitions and materials at their own risk."

July 29, 1940

The Act of Havana

This act, chaired by the venerable, highly respected U.S. Secretary of State Cordell Hull at the Pan American Conference in Havana Cuba and attended by representatives of South American countries and other Pan American States, was a ground breaking Act of far more significance and importance than its name would imply!

In conception, it was like that of our "Continental Congress:" Its proposed enactments were made in much the same vein, and for similar purposes, as those of our "Articles of Confederation." The proposed new community of administration and control, the "Inter-American Commission of Territorial Administration," though less detailed and less restrictive in nature had an administrative-defining role in a much comparable way, to that of our U.S. Congress.

Looking at it all, from the mellowing less detailed perspective of time, one can't help but muse: "Sounds much like long-ago thoughts for the beginnings of an United States of South America."

Many of the Pan American nations were considered to be the colonial possessions of Germany, Italy and others of its "Axis" partners who were then at war with England and were doing all they could to get help from their satellite countries and extend their Nazi doctrines and control.

The purpose of this Pan American conference was to make sure that this would not happen to any of their members.

After much debate and haggling, particularly by Argentina, they finally came to an agreement:

The following is a listing of major agreements and stipulations reached at this Act of Havana Conference:

- Establish a provisional administration of government under the surveillance of a new "Inter-American Commission of Territorial Administration" which shall be composed of one representative for each of the ratifying states.

- The (existing) sovereignty of one non-American (foreign) State to another non-American (foreign) State, thereby threatening the peace of the continent, (cannot be allowed except with the consent of a regime of provisional administration).
- Forced Labor shall be abolished.
- Local laws and customs must be respected to the extent possible.
- Provide means to improve education, health and wealth.
- Natives of existing communities shall operate under their own charters and customs.
- The new administration shall continue for a term of three years.

August 18, 1940

Hemispheric Defence.

President Roosevelt and Prime Minister Mackenzie King of Canada, met at Ogdensburg New York to discuss mutual problems of defence and agreed to a Permanent Joint Board on defence to study the readiness status of sea, land and air forces.

September 2, 1940

Exchange of U.S. Navy Destroyers for British Air and Naval Bases.

Through an exchange of letters between U.S. Secretary of State, Cordell Hull, and the British Representative, the Marques of Lothian, the United States agreed to the immediate transfer of eighty "flush-deck," "four pipe" type destroyers from the Navy in exchange for a ninety-nine year lease of numerous British naval and air bases located in the Bahamas, St. Lucia, Trinidad, Gulf of Persia, Antigua and British Guana.

A poll taken at the end of 1940 showed that more than 80% of

Americans did not want to get involved in the war in Europe. There were enough problems of our own right here at home.

January 6, 1941

F.D.R.'s "Four Freedoms Speech" in his annual address to Congress.

This speech has been hailed by the people of America throughout the years, as a proud statement of who we are and what we stand for.

Before reiterating pertinent parts of this speech "verbatim," let me first jot down a few lines of his eloquent address to Congress that preceded it:

"...Every realist knows that the democratic way of life is, at this moment, being directly assailed in every part of the world—assailed either by the force of arms or by the spreading of propaganda..."

"...I find it necessary to report that the future and safety of our country, and of our democracy, are overwhelmingly involved in events far beyond our borders."

"...In times like these it is immature—and incidentally untrue—for anybody to brag that an unprepared America, single handed, and with one hand tied behind its back, can hold off the whole world."

"...Those who would give up essential liberty to purchase a little temporary safety deserves neither liberty nor safety."

Now for the Four Freedoms:

- "The first is freedom of speech and expression—everywhere in the world."
- "The second is freedom of every person to worship God in how own way—everywhere in the world."
- "The third is freedom from want—which translated into world terms, means economic understanding which will secure to every nation a healthy peace-time life for its inhabitants—everywhere in the world."
- "The fourth is freedom from fear—which, translated into world terms, means a world-wide reduction of armaments to such a point, and in such a thorough fashion that no nation will be in a position to commit an act of physical aggression

against any neighbor—anywhere in the world."

Third Administration, Franklin D. Roosevelt (1941-[49?]

Jan 20, 1941: After the most one-sided presidential victory in history (by an electoral vote of 449 to 82) Roosevelt and new Vice President, Henry A. Wallace (his former Secretary of Agriculture) takes the oath of office and assumes the Presidency of the United States for the third time.

Roosevelt's defeated Republican opponent, Wendell Willkie, was a personable, well-liked attorney and businessman from Indiana, and also a veteran of World War I. It was no disgrace to have lost the "race" even by such an overwhelming margin. Who else in those hard, unsettled times could have done much better against the eloquence and untiring work for "the people" as F.D.R., his opponent!

Willkie was a good person, and a good speaker too—I know; (as a growing-up young lad in those days I had listened to a few of his radio speeches when I lived in Traverse City, Michigan). And Roosevelt admired and recognized Willkie too. And the two became good friends.[16*] "During World War 2, Willkie supported Roosevelt's Lend Lease Program to Britain, promoted an organization to protect world peace and fought to improve civil liberties in the U.S.A. In 1942, Roosevelt named him "good-will ambassador" to the Middle East, China and the Soviet Union. His 1943 book "*One World,*" was a best seller."

March 11, 1941

The Land Lease Act of 1941

[16*] Ref: The Cambridge Biographical Encyclopedia, pg. 1,000.

Following the earlier verbal accords on this subject reached by the U.S. Secretary of State, Cordell Hull and the British representative, The Marques of Lothian, a "Land Lease" bill, embodying the intent of the agreement, with minor changes, was forwarded to Congress.

After heated debate, much of it in an obvious disregard of prior neutrality legislation, it was finally, (resentfully by many) approved and became law.

No question now about our commitment to Britain and the allied cause!

August 9-14, 1941

The Atlantic Charter

This was a very historic meeting in a very dramatic setting: Franklin Delano Roosevelt, President of the United States on the Heavy Cruiser, *U.S.S. Augusta*, flagship of the U.S. Atlantic Fleet; and Sir Winston (Leonard Spencer) Churchill, Prime Minister of England aboard the British battleship *H.M.S. Prince of Wales*, in Argentia Harbor, on the south coast of Newfoundland.

The accord they agreed to, was momentous too. (Pardon me if you will, but there seems to have been more than a little touch of Shakespeare in the aura of it all).

The objectives to which we of the "free world" aspire in this big battle of clashing international philosophies was spelled-out in the following list:

The Atlantic Charter:

1. We seek no aggrandizement, territorial or otherwise.
2. We seek no territorial changes not given freely by the wishes of the people concerned.
3. We respect the right of all people to choose their own form of government; Sovereign rights restored to those who have been forcefully deprived of them.
4. Access of all peoples on equal terms to trade; and access to the raw materials their economies need.

5. Improve labor standards, economic advancement, and social security.
6. After destruction of Nazi tyranny, establish a peace which shall afford to all nations, safety in their own boundaries, and freedom from fear and want.
7. A peace that shall enable all men to traverse the high seas and oceans without hindrance.
8. Abandon all use of force to the extent possible. Disarmament to would-be aggressors. And encourage all measures which shall lead to the maintenance of peace.

September 1941

Another poll taken in September, 1941, showed that Americans were now "fed up with the spreading incursions of the Japanese in the Far East and in the Pacific. Nearly 70% now felt that efforts to stop those incursions was now worth the risk of going to war!

That resolve would be tested in a big way, soon!

December 7, 1941

"Day of Infamy"

Fighters and bombers from an undetected Japanese fleet roar into just awakening Pearl Harbor at sunrise and create havoc, while the unsuspecting sailors were "making morning colors" on their ships. And soldiers, sailors, and airmen barracked in nearby Hickman and Honolulu itself were busily running up their "colors" too.

And the damage was devastating, particularly to the ships tied up to the berths along Battleship Row and to the fighters and bombers lined up, in indefensible neat rows at nearby airfields. And to their suddenly awakened crews who struggled valiantly to fight back to save them—but didn't have a chance.

The word got out fast. And momentous happenings took place one after another:

December 8, 1941, Roosevelt stood before Congress; declared war on Japan and labelled their dastardly acts of the day before as their

"Day of Infamy."

December 11, 1941

Germany and Italy declare war on the United States.

Roosevelt and Congress reciprocate and declare war on Germany and Italy that same day.

The United States was now in one big war for sure! And we went to work with a fervor to avenge what had happened. And hopefully make sure that it couldn't happen again—at least in our time.

And the Great Depression quickly faded into memory.

CHAPTER IIG

Desperate Journey

AT THIS point, before the end of our story, let's now take a little trip back in time (and in memory to some of us) to those long-ago days of the "Great Depression" and do a little reminiscing on its effects on our daily lives and how we "made do to make it through."

I'll try to be brief.

When I think of those rough times, I think of how difficult it must have been for my dear mother and father too. As I mentioned before, we moved all around this land to try to find a way to survive.

After California and Pennsylvania and Ohio, we "picked up stakes" and moved on (by a 1½ ton stake-bodied truck) to Kentucky, the land of Dad's boyhood.

There we took up residence, for a while, in a little three-room log cabin, by the side of the Bardstown Highway, just to the South of the little village of Fern Creek.

On a nearby slope was the little white-steepled church called "Fairmont Chapel." Though abandoned for some time, Dad—who was an ordained minister—opened it up and became its "preacher."

How proud we all were to listen to his sermons—particularly the one on "Mother's Day." What fun it was on Sunday mornings to pull on the rope that rang the bell in the steeple!

But money is seldom the reason for being in the ministry. It is usually the "calling" to do something good for the other person, that drives good men on. And this, for sure, was the case for Dad. He tried all sorts of things to try to make a living. One of these was selling "Rawleigh" products door-to-door. At other times it was bagging potatoes and working in the fields. And often, on the weekends, my younger brother Bill and I would be there in the fields beside him.

At home our dear mother would be washing our clothes by hand on a washboard in a tub—and wringing them out by hand—and toting them out to a clothesline between two trees to dry. One day we discovered that "choke weeds" (I believe this is the right description) were almost as good as spinach. So mother would boil the ones we found, in a pot hung on a hook above the fire in our open fireplace. To be honest, they really were pretty good.

When fall came around and it was time to go back to school, a school bus would pick me up from in front of our cabin and take me away to freshman classes in Fern Creek High.

Of all the schools I have ever been in—and believe me, in my time there were plenty!—I can think of none with more fondness than those days at Fern Creek High. What wonderful understanding friends I have never in all of my school days met any better.

To top it off, I often was in the same study hall with my beautiful first cousin Elsie Farmer. Though our paths diverted through all of the years, we have kept in touch as best of friends. During my years at sea—during WWII, her letters "from home" about the doings of her farm and her husband Leo Deutsch—who I also knew—sure brightened the day and were reminders that the whole world hadn't gone crazy and that compassion and the precepts of love for one another—often hidden by the frenzy—were still to be found if we would only try to see.

Then one day a loaded down little car towing a tiny little house trailer stopped in front of our cabin. Then introducing himself, the tired worn-out driver got out and asked if he and his also weary wife could park under the trees by the side of our house for the night. They had been on the road for many days and were so tired, they could hardly see.

Then with "Certainly, we know what you've been through," Dad took him by the hand; showed him where to park and with "By the way it won't be too fancy. But why don't you also come to dinner!" We didn't realize it at the time but thus began a big turning point in the lives and fortunes of our family.

The next morning our visitors were gone. But what they had told us would affect our lives dramatically forever.

Finding work all around the country was next to impossible. Everywhere you went people were starving for the want of just a little to eat. Others were "shivering to death" in cardboard boxes and under blankets of newspapers in the alleys and crannies of the cities where they went to seek shelter in the cold, cold nights.

But maybe—just perhaps—there might be an "out;" A way to survive—for those who were willing to move to another part of the country and work real hard and spend long hours doing strange new work that most had never done before.

The growing season of the year was now over. Time now to harvest the crops in many parts of this country. Rumor had it that up north in places like Michigan, the growers and farmers of crops, such as cherries and beans, and even strawberries, just might need extra hands—for a time at least—to help out.

Also, when that was over, there just might be a chance for work in one of the canning companies in the area that processed and packaged the crops—at least for a time. Nowhere else, it seemed, was there work to be had. It was better than freezing to death or starving. It was worth a try.

A week or so later, after trading the truck for a 1928 Buick and a trailer and saying good-bye to our friends and relatives, the Farmers, our family of seven[17*] piled into the car and headed north with our worldly possessions (including a tent) trailing along behind.

Looking back to that long ago time we must have seemed remark-

---

17* Listed by age: Father, Mother, myself, Bill, Marjory, Janie, & little brother Tom.

ably similar to the "Joads" in Steinbeck's "Grapes of Wrath." And, in truth, our circumstances really were in many ways. And many, many others in those terrible days were faced with the very same problems and make-shift solutions. And had to do things and make decisions that in "normal" times would be frowned-on as absurd and asinine. But, those were the times "that tried men's souls," and most who have never been faced with the plethora of economic and social and emotional forces involved in just trying to "make do" and survive in the conditions that were endemic in the "Great Depression," simply have no "inkling" of what the depth of the description "horrible" for those times, really truly implies. —R.F.H.

Well, our trip to the north was one to be long remembered. In truth it was a trip to the unknown and at times, when we gave it some thought, it was really scary. And at times I thought to myself: "I wonder what it would be like if I could transpose myself now to ten years later in the future."

The Bardstown Highway and route 31 were the same and fortunately according to the map, if we stayed on 31 it would take us all of the way. And with little traffic on the roads, in those days, the going was rather easy. It wasn't long before we were through the little town of Buechel, then Louisville itself. Then, crossing the bridge over the "Falls of the Ohio," we were suddenly in Indiana. It was easy going. The long ribbon of road ahead was clear; the purrings of our Buick were hypnotic. As Roosevelt had stated: "We had nothing to fear but fear itself." So, reservations and concerns abated (or put on the "back burner" to be more accurate) we settled back in the ambience of the moment, and the adventure of it all, the best we could.

Then suddenly the engine sputtered and coughed to a stop. Dad pulled over to the side of the road and raised the hood. The vacuum tank,[18*] that sucked fuel (via a vacuum) from the gasoline tank at the rear of a vehicle and fed into the engine under the hood, was bone dry.

Not knowing what else to do, and fortunate to have a long enough hose of the right size (perhaps it was a standard piece of "emergency equipment" to carry along in those days), Dad siphoned gas from the gasoline tank at the rear of the car and refilled the vacuum tank.

It worked! That is, until the problem and its temporary solution repeated themselves every twenty or so miles later.

What "ambience" for our adventure we may have felt at the start was by now long gone. And we were more than a little worried.

Then a knowing attendant at a gas station along the way knew the answer.

"Why, friend," he pointed out, "Look at the cap of your gas tank: it doesn't have a hole!" And you know—he was right! Then after taking it off and punching a hoe in it with a nail and hammer, and screwing it back in place, he called out "Now try it." And by golly that sweet little engine returned to life and believe me there were more smiles and sighs of relief all over the place. And that proud attendant deserved all of the plaudits and "thanks," and more, that we could think of at the time. And even now, years later, in memory. And, you know: the well-known parable about "For the want of a nail" seems to have more than just a little authenticity to it now when I think of the story of the long-ago Buick that was wanting a hole in its gas cap.

The more I look back at the timing and the details of this "desperate journey" that took place more than sixty-seven years ago, the more I am amazed at how much courage my parents must have had to set out on such a tenuous venture with so little means and so questionable an outcome. Everything in the world they owned was now with them—the bank crash of '29 made sure of that.

If the crops had been already picked and there were no jobs

18* In the "old days," before the advent of mechanical fuel pumps, vacuum tanks were used to "suck" gasolene from the gasolene tank & store it close to the engine.

ahead—our funds were nearly exhausted—there would be no way to turn back. Only heaps of good fortune or "divine intervention," it seemed, could then save the day.

But there were jobs along the way. And at the end too! And we were welcomed!

The fields of Niles and gardens of Benton Harbor were lush with beans and strawberries, and other vegetables the names of which I have long forgotten. And we were welcome to have them for our own meals if we wished. And believe me, we did!

When night came we could often pitch our little tent. At one time we were welcome t o use a little grainery. At others there might be a little cabin. But we didn't care. It wasn't bad at all. At least we were surviving and we were doing it with honor, the best way we knew how.

Then, the fields to the south now picked, we piled into the car and headed north to our destination, Traverse City.

The outskirts of South Haven and Holland and Muskegon went by as we wended our way. Then a jog to the right to the little town of Scottville. And on to Manistee; and another jog to the right at Honor.

We stopped and rested for a while by the wayside; we were nearing the end. And the closer we got, the greater were our reservations for the path we had chosen, and our concerns for what may lay ahead.

But it was too late to change now. Then getting back in our seats—and mentally crossing our fingers—we headed on through sleepy little Grawn.

Then suddenly, there it was before us: Traverse City, Michigan: The city of twelve thousand happy souls living in a beautiful array of well-kept homes and lawns and gardens within the bordering frames of sidewalks and tree-lined roads. To top it all off, it's white, sandy beaches to the north, were snuggled by two big, blue freshwater bays.

And all about there were lakes full of bluegills and sunfish, and perch, and bass. And there were deer and bear roaming woods all about that seemed to go on and on forever. "A true gem of the North" we thought to ourselves then—and still do today.

But to us, all was lost if Dad couldn't find a job—and soon!

We were truly at the end of the survival road. Dad had only thirty-five cents left in his pockets!

So we pulled up to the Cherry Growers Canning Company on Front Street, and Dad crossed the street, opened the door, and went in.

Not a word was said in our car as we waited—one of the most stressful, important waits of our lives.

Then suddenly the front door of cherry Growers opened. And Dad was there. And he was smiling! He got the job! And he would begin tomorrow. Better yet, Mr. Hollister, a new-found friend (and now fellow worker) had a small farm on Garfield Road and he had invited us to pitch our tent near his home and stay until we were settled.

Yes, there really is a Santa Clause! And he comes in many guises—and often when you least expect him.

The rest is now history. I've already told you some of it: school in Traverse City High; meeting Ralph Vanderley and later his future wife Teresa; and through their friendship my beloved future wife Clarice.

One thing for sure though, Mr. Hollister (and his family who would become wonderful friends) and the Traverse City Canning Company (that saved the day) will be long remembered by all in that 1928 Buick, who so anxiously waited outside for the life-changing answer on that long-ago day in the "Great Depression."

CHAPTER IIH

The Deep South and the Appalachians; Noah Meets Sally

ONE MORE story and I'll be through. This one about the "Deep South" and my sister Marjory and her husband, Norman Chaviers Sr., and his family before, during and after the Great Depression.

In a very real way, it's a story of later-day pioneers who worked the land—often by hand, horses and mules—in and around the rolling, often craggy, hills of the Appalachians.

They loved gospel music, and regularly went to church on Sundays—even if it meant going there, sometimes, barefoot and often in rags.

To them, self-sufficiency was a way of life. To lend a helping hand to a "brother" was a reason for being.

And though (Norman tells me) they were often "as poor as mice," they were at peace with the bounty of love and friendship that was all around and they never ever felt that they were anything but rich.

Norman's father, Noah William Chaviers was born not far to the west of Chattanooga, Tennessee near the meandering Tennessee River and Walden Ridge of the Appalachians. Later they moved a little south to Fort Payne, Alabama, near the edge of Lookout Mountain.

Later still, Noah Chaviers—by now an average size man with a warm heart and a jovial disposition—decided to set out on his own and see what he could do. "First" stop: Boaz, a quaint little city on a plateau of Sand Mountain whose main street in those days—I am told—was only "about two blocks long."

Noah liked it so much that he stayed for the rest of his life.

But this isn't the end of our story—yet. The Great Depression would soon set in.

How Noah and his soon-to-be young family, and others all around, would ride it out, "Appalachian Style" is, I believe you'll agree, an intriguing, eye-opening story.

I'll try to tell it, as it was related to me to the best of my limited knowledge of the details.

Well, time went on, and after staying at the home of one of his brothers, who was already there, until he was "settled," he set out to find work and a place he could call his own.

Finding work at this time of the year wasn't all that difficult; the nearby cotton mill seemed to always need workers. And nearby farms, it seemed, could almost always use help. But a "place of his own"—that would take a bit more doing! Not only did the "right spot of land" have to be available. The price must be right and it had to be just what he needed and had in mind.

One day, after heaps of looking around, Noah finally came across a sixty or so acre piece of land with an unoccupied "ram shackled" three-room wooden house, with a barn and sheds to match, that had possibilities.

Then, seeking out the owner he asked what it would take to but it.

"Well, I'll tell ya, " said the obviously interested "landlord." "'Taint for sale. But you can lease it, 'as is,' if you stay on it and put the land to use and give me part of the profits."

Noah happily agreed. And their handshakes sealed the bargain. And in the doing, Noah became a "share cropper."

The enormity of what now lay ahead and what he must do before he could move in and work the land hadn't escaped him.

But that is why he had come! And that is what his father and father's father and many others before them had done—in many ways for him. And darned if he'd even think of letting them down—now that he was able to pick up the reins.

First the run-down house must be cleaned up and repaired to make it habitable. And a table and chairs must be found or made. And the list went on: Kerosene lamps (& kerosene too) and pots and pans and, oh yes, a bed and bedding.

And for a farmer, the list went on and on: plows and scythes and hoes and rakes.

And most importantly there must be seeds for the corn fields and cotton fields and seeds for the tomatoes and cabbages and yams and squash in the garden. And for the cane that would later be squeezed for its syrup.

What a long, long list of things to do! But let's not forget the livestock: the horse, and perhaps a mule, to work the field and pull the wagon. And the chickens—that with dumplings and pone—would make delicious meals. And their eggs that were as "good as gold" and would sell for five cents each from the peddler with his "Rolling Store." (But more about that later).

What a tremendous job lay ahead! For sure" Noah would be mighty busy!

But, you know! He was "up to the task," and more.

Then one day, after he and the blacksmith had built him a wagon, he hitched up his new team of horses, said "Thanks, see you later" to his brother and clip-clopped away a few miles down the pike to the place that, for many long years to come, he would be proud to call "home."

But gosh! Being alone sure was awful lonely! And there just happened to be a pretty, little raven-haired girl on a near-by farm that he had noticed quite often. And, once in a while, she'd wave hello and smile back at him as he passed her way.

"Perhaps. Yes, perhaps—it might be well if he'd give her a little more thought."

And it wasn't long before he did. And it was obvious that she liked him and thought of him too.

And they'd often go on wagon rides together, and to Sunday meetings at church.

And one day, on a walk by a nearby stream, Noah took her in his arms and, with a pounding heart and strangely trembling voice, asked if she'd be his bride. Then, with a roguish toss of her raven locks and an impish grin, that he'd always remember, Sally Freeman answered: "Yes my darling—till the end of time—thought you'd never ask!"

And the years rolled by. What a wonderful joyous family they raised! Four boys and four girls. Of the boys, Norman tells me, "he was number two."

And though so many are now gone,[19*] such wonderful memories remain!

Let's go back in time now, if you will, and revisit, for a while, a few of those memories as they were told to me.

But before going on, it would be well to point out that when we talk about memories, it isn't always about those we cherish. There are memories too, about things we abhorred and weren't so nice.

Life, we all know, is a mixture of both. And to have the first we must know and rise above the latter. And, in the knowing of both, we gain a perspective that reveals true worth and guides us on our way.

Take a glimpse of their daily lives and we can pick some of these out together:

---

19 * Along with their father, Noah, and their mother, Sally, all of the boys except Norman (George, "J.L.," and Ray) are now with their "Maker" in the "Great Beyond." All of the sisters—what beautiful names they have—are still with us today: Edith Monel, Bobbie Jean, Tressie Faye, and Betty Ann.

CHAPTER IIJ

Though Things Were Scarce, Never Once Did They Feel They Were "Poor."

THERE WAS no electricity for miles around. Only oil lamps to see by at night and in the shadows of the day. And, though some had reflectors, it wasn't easy to read and study and do the chores that had to be done in the dimness of the flickering light. But though it wasn't easy, there was a closeness about it all that no money in the world could buy. And is still there today among those who are still with us and are doing what they can to carry on.

And telephones—"there wasn't one" (well maybe just one) for miles around. My brother-in-law, Norman, who—like me—is now in his eighties) didn't see one until he was an airman at Scott Field, Illinois in '43 during WWII.[20*]

Automobiles! What were those? There was nary a one in town either.

And when one did honk and rattle its way through on the gravely road to somewhere, the shopkeepers and the blacksmith, and others who had heard about these things, quickly turned out and held on to their tethered horses until this "talk of the day" and its grinning driver had finally, safely passed through.

Norman tells me that living on his farm, a short distance away, he

---

20* My mother Marjory (by then a widow) was also at Scott Field, teaching radio to "her boys" in the U.S. Air Corps at the time. It is also through this connection that my sister, Marjory May, and Norman eventually met. (More about this a little later).

had never seen a car until he was a teenager.

And there were other things that were non-existent, or in short supply for all at the time:

No central sanitation systems; outhouses "adorned" the landscape most everywhere. Hospitals, it seems, were few and far between. And schools? There was a grade school called "Carlyle" that stood all alone by the side of the gravel road, three miles south of Mountainboro.

And a High School a little closer (5 miles away) in Sardis. Not convenient when you had to get there on your own! Particularly when your only transportation was by horse and wagon.

There was another big problem: going to school was secondary when you were needed to work in the fields!

As a result, Norman's early school work suffered, but he made up for it in a big way later, after he had left the farm and was on his own.

Throughout history, as far as we know, living off the land has never been easy. In almost everything man has done, and still must do, from the preparation of the earth to its planting and caring and gleaning, there are many challenges of nature that must be met and overcome: Flood and drought; heat and cold; sunshine and gloom; tempest and calm—all play a giant part and must be anticipated and faced. And, improvisation—often on short notice—is sometimes the only way to get by and survive.

In the Appalachians, where Noah and Sally and their eight children lived, improvisation with what they had, was an accepted way of life.

And they did it well and with a will! And there were many "fun things" to do and take part in along the way to buoy up their spirit. And many friends to remind them that they were not alone.

And, as "Marge" and Norman now frequently remind me: "Though they may have lacked many material things, they always managed to 'get-by.' Never, ever did they feel they were 'poor!'"

And not having everything, there was much to look forward to. And when good things did arrive or happen it was like syrup on their corn pone and sure “made their day”—and also, such wonderful memories—for times jut like now!

CHAPTER IIK

More Appalachian Memories

THIS IS a good time, I believe, to delve into a few of those memories:

Some are amusing; some are surprising, and some are surprisingly quite ordinary. But all are revealing of how people lived and what they did to get by and enjoy life to its fullest possible in places called "Horseshoe Bend," "Goodwater," "Jackson Gap," "Kowaliga," and—oh yes—"Boaz, Alabama," in the Appalachian Mountains and nearby areas of the "Deep South," before, during, and after the years of the "Great Depression."

Norm now tells me that they were so poor in those days that "even the mice, who sometimes sneaked in, would bring their own lunches!"

And when winter came and they woke up in the cold, cold mornings, there would often be snow on the top of their blankets as it breezed-in through the cracks in their walls.

Also, the gaps in the boards of their raised wooden floors were so wide that you could often see the huddled-together chickens below that had scooted their way there to get out of the weather.

Getting water for wash-up, and later for breakfast, was another unenviable experience in the cold winter days. Particularly if you were the first up (or the one first elected) and were still in your "long johns."

It was a memorable experience that you wanted to get over fast:

First order of the day—shovel a path through the snow and around the drifts to the little house-like cupola over the forty-foot deep hand dug well.

Once there, turn the crank of the rope-wound wooden spindle to lower the attached bucket to the water below.

Then, bucket full, turn the crank the other way to rewind the rope and bring the bucket up.

Not really a difficult process at all. But it was the getting to it in the cold early mornings (when you were often in your "skivvies") that negated all illusions of glamour and urged you not to tarry and get of with this little task fast!

Just before spring rolled around it was suddenly "clothes for the year time" for the children. An exciting time for all. First the children lined up standing on a large piece of cardboard on the floor. Then, one-by-one, Noah would trace around the soles of their shoes with a pencil to record their sizes. This would then be taken with the children to Dobson's Dry Goods Store (now long gone) in Boaz where shoes for all and clothing for the boys would be purchased (or ordered if they were not on hand).

Clothes for the girls would be cut-out by Sally from decorative fertilizer sacks and hand-sewn by her on her treadle sewing machine.

The years supply for the boys was strictly adhered to and consisted of the following items: one pair of shoes, two pairs of socks, two shirts, two jackets and two pairs of "long-handled" underwear each.

If, during the year, some should be ripped or torn, well—money was scarce and rules were rules. It would be best that they be sewn-up or patched if at all possible.

Norman tells me that abiding by this rule could sometimes lead to embarrassing moments:

Once when he had just ripped the seat of his pants so badly that "you could almost see daylight," two ladies, in all of their finery, suddenly appeared when he was walking down the street, and casually, unknowingly walked his way.

In much distress and to hide the nature of his plight, he turned around when they had passed, and walked backwards until they were "safely" out of sight.

Not much of a story, I guess. But there were other implications: a bad ending to an event such as this—and the snickers and grins and guffaws that might follow—could really play hob with a person's composure! Perhaps even end a guy's good day—

Preparing the fields in the Spring was a prideful, generally one man with a team of horses operation. Turning over the earth with a plow and smoothing its lumps—with a chain-held log behind a strong, responsive team that followed your every "gee-haw" command just had to be exhilarating. Particularly when you knew that this was the first step in the process that would assure for your family it's daily bread for the year. And you were the one in charge!

Other work in the fields such as seeding, weeding and the like were usually shared by all when needed. Particularly when it was time to harvest the corn and cotton.

My sister, Marjory, who moved to Alabama after her marriage to Norman and was a willing (even eager) participant in the activities of her new-found family, has always been quick to point out that the times "pulling corn" and "picking cotton[21*]" on "their" farm with his laughing, joking sisters were "the best times of her life—ever." And if time could be rolled back and they could all be together again, she'd

21 * Picking cotton was done with your bare hands (no gloves). A long fabric bag with a loop on the open end was looped around your neck and under one shoulder then dragged behind on the ground. Each cotton boll contained four sections (in the manner of an orange). The white or yellowish soft, wool-like substance in the middle was "pulled" by hand from the sharp-pointed, tough outer covering called the "burrs." You had to be careful in handling the bolls. It's sharp pointed burrs could prick your fingers and cause much pain.

"do it, again, in a minute!"

By the time Norman was in his mid-teens, motorized vehicles, of various descriptions, began to make their appearance in the area.

Of particular interest to all in the family, including Noah and Sally, was the arrival of the peddler's "Rolling Store:" A mechanized, van-like, contraption (with cages underneath to store traded chickens) began to make the rounds of the farms every few weeks.

It's arrival was much anticipated. Not only were there dry goods for sale, such as flour and spices (and perhaps a few pots and pans too), you didn't always have to pay in cash! You could trade with chickens or eggs. Or sell to the peddler outright. And the eggs you could sell were carefully handled. At five cents a piece they were valued like gold!

Later in t he year, when the days were shorter and there was a bite to the increasingly chilly air, the man with the horse-drawn "squeezing machine" would drop by to squeeze the sweet sap out of their recently harvested sugar cane.

Like the "Rolling Store," it's coming was very welcome. And all would gather around to feed this interesting machine and watch its progress.

In construction, it was a rather simple machine. But also, in a way, quite ingenious. Sort of like an old-time, hand-cranked clothes wringer. Except the rollers were vertical and of steel. And the turning handle at the top was much, much longer and was turned, around and around (like a merry-go-round) by a horse and bridle.

Feeding the machine wasn't all that hard. Just a case of guiding bundles of newly-cut cane through a hole in one side of the tank through the turning rollers. Then out, through a matching hole in the other side, came the newly squeeze-dried stalks.

The reward was at the bottom! A constant stream of sweet sap (soon to be syrup) made the exit through a tap, to a hose and then to a myriad of eagerly waiting buckets.

Boy, in the coming cold winter mornings would hot sweet corn syrup doused on piles of pancakes just off the griddle, taste good!

Though they never had toys that were bought when they were children, and seldom candy, Christmas and the good times they all shared, made up for it in a big way!

As night time fell on Christmas Eve, if you awoke, you would see rows of knitted stockings hanging on hooks on the fireplace mantel.

When morning came, a seemingly miraculous thing had happened: They were all filled with oranges and apples and nuts (and of all things!) sticks of hard candy. And the love and joy of their being shone in the happy faces gathered around!

No better Christmas mornings have they ever had since!

Then off to the Baptist Church in their Sunday-go-to-meeting best. Then there they would meet old friends and hold their hands. And the rafters would ring with the powerful sounds of the organ and the beautifully sung words of "The Old Rugged Cross," "I'll Fly Away," "I'll Meet You in the Morning," and so many other, well-remembered, never-to-be-forgotten hymns that would fill the air!

Christmas Dinner—well that was something else! Every good, tasty thing there was to eat—or could ever think of—I am told—was there: Roast chicken and turkey and ham; hot corn bread and dumplings; heaping bowls of mashed potatoes—with yummy frying pan gravy. Ham and sugared yams, hot biscuits just out of the oven to be smothered with sweet tasting home churned butter.

What a feast!

And, you know: just thinking of it all makes me hungry—and I wasn't even there!

There are two more things I'd like to talk about before concluding this story of the Appalachians and bringing an end to this book:

The first is a return to the Appalachians, for a short time, to put conditions there during the Great Depression in perspective.

The second, and last, if you don't mind, I'd like to take you with me for a brief trip back in time, to Belleville, Illinois and the beautiful, fortunate day of World War II when my beautiful little sister Marjory and handsome Corporal Norman W. Chaviers, of the nearby Scott

Field Air Force Base, first met. It was a meeting they both tell me that just had to have been arranged by God!

CHAPTER IIL

Riding Out the Hard Times with Courage and a Lot of Improvisation.

AS I have related before about the Great Depression: pain and sorrow, hopelessness and despair ruled the land and nearly all who lived init. "Today" was but a hopeless struggle; a "Better tomorrow" was naught but a hoped-for illusion.

But, though almost everyone (including millions of others throughout the world) suffered its consequences, some were able to ride them out better than others. Where and how they lived, and the lessons passed on by others who had lived there before them played a big part in how they were able to adapt to the degrading conditions and cope.

Based on first had knowledge from trusted friends and loved ones who lived there at the time (and still do) I now firmly, truly believe that Noah and Sally and their family who once lived as "share croppers" on a then-remote Sand Mountain plateau of the Southern Appalachians, near the now bustling little city of Boaz, Alabama, did indeed represent the legendary "can do" American spirit that was so sorely needed everywhere at the time.

Sure, it certainly wasn't easy: the farms didn't always provide all they needed. Though they were never hungry and never really cold, trading with eggs and chickens and vegetables from the garden [didn't] always "do the trick." When there were clothes to buy and coal oil for the lamps, and you needed new parts or equipment, you had to have real money.

So, often, when the weather allowed and the jobs were available, Noah worked on whatever jobs he could find at the time, like almost everyone else.

And, though working from dawn to dusk on roads and bridges for the W.P.A. and the county, paid only fifty cents a day. It was enough. With care and planning it bought what was needed. And he never complained.

Now, Noah and Sally are gone—and others of their wonderful family too—their "can do spirit" and love for one another and respect for their fellow man is a shining example. And still lives on in those who have proudly, quietly picked up the banner and still carry on today!

My sister "Marge"[22*] and her husband Norman who now live in a modest, brick-sided home on church Street (what an appropriate name) in Boaz, Alabama have done many wonderful things for others in peril: adopted several sons; cared for my aging mother, Marjory, and my blind brother Tom during the last years of their lives. Even today when I call them on the phone (and I must admit I do it often) our conversations will be interrupted when their door bell rings and there is someone asking if they still have free food to give them from the pantry they keep, just for that purpose, in a room in their house.

22* Marjory (or Marge as we all now her) was one of those two little girls in this story who rode in the 1928 Buick on its "desperate journey" north during those long-ago days of the "Great Depression." She is also the one, who in years gone by, was sometimes, playfully, proudly pointed-out by the Southern-bred Noah, as his "Damn Yankee Daughter-in-law."

CHAPTER IIM

Marge & Norman—Two Ships that Blinked in the Night.

A LITTLE word, a little smile, a little nod-of -the-head can make such a difference! Like two ships passing unobserved in the night until one of them blinks a light.

Such was the case of how Marge and Norman first met.

How it happened and the changes it made to their lives is a captivating love story:

After Dad died, and I was at sea during the war years (WWII), Mother and the rest of our family were left to get by on their own. And, except for a small monthly allotment from me (which the government matched) they had no income.

Fortunately mother and dad had both been studying radio at one of the colleges in or near St. Louis, Missouri, before, as part of the war effort. This saved the day! She was assigned to teach what she had learned, to newly arrived airmen at the Scott Field Airbase on the other side of the Mississippi River in Illinois. While there she rented a house in a small community not far from Scott Field and the nearby city of Belleville where my sister, Marjory, continued her high school studies.

Proud to say, my sisters Marjory and Janie were attractive young ladies and had beautiful voices to match. They were often called upon to sing together at school events. A few times in the summers they would continue to sing duets on a stern-wheel riverboat to entertain the passengers as it wended it's picturesque way up and down the "old Mississippi" River.

To further enhance my feelings of pride for my sisters, I just have to add two more comments: years before, when Marjory was a little girl in Cleveland, Ohio, she used to be the model for an artist who drew up the designs for Shirley Temple dolls and cut outs!

In later years Janie, who had a beautiful, powerful voice, sang once in a while in country music bands. And boy could she yodel!

Now the interesting part of this story: How these "two ships in the night," Marjory and Norman, first met.

Well its short and simple and it goes like this:

Norman had joined up with the Army Air Corps sometime near the end of World War II, and took Basic Training at Wichita Falls, Texas.

Then later to Scott Field, Illinois where he was a Corporal specializing in radio repair.

It was a cool spring day in May 1946. The celebrated movie, "Stars and Stripes Forever" was playing in nearby Belleville. Norm and an Air Force "buddy" decided they would like to go into town to see it.

So when the next bus came along, they hopped aboard and headed that way.

At about the same time in a little town, also near Belleville, Marjory and a high school girl friend boarded their bus and headed that way too.

Fortunately for the present posterity, both buses arrived at the bus stop near the theatre at the same time and began to unload.

As soon a Marge came into view, Norman exclaimed to himself: Wow!

Then, when their paths to the theatre had merged, he called out to that "girl of his dreams" who was suddenly beside him: "Hi beautiful!" Marge looked up in surprise; liked what she saw; and they walked in to see the movie together. The rest is history!

They were married October 4, 1946. Their first child, Norman Jr. was born in Belleville about a year later.

Now, after sixty-one years of happy marriage, and a "passel" of wonderful children and grandchildren, Norman now tells me: "Guess this marriage *will* last!"

CHAPTER IIN

Reflections

HOW DIFFERENT things are today: Boaz is much, much larger. And the roads are all paved. And those passing through are many lanes wider. And the vehicles on them are seldom alone: Passenger cars race through, one after another. And the "semi's," several trailers long, are often in caravans.

But this is not to criticize. It is the way things are; the way they have evolved.

"Would we want to go back to the 'good old days?'" Well, we'd have to think that one over a lot.

But then again, there is many a lonely heart that silently cries: "Dear God, if I could only go back to visit those wonderful times again—just once more!"

But there is another distinction that must be made. I and many others of the "Great Depression/WWII" era have lived through the gamut of some of the worst of times and some of the best of times ever! In the normal divergences of living, we have trod many different paths in many different ways to sometimes, many different objectives since. And in the process of trying to succeed and do our best, we have gained many varying perspectives. And though we may not always agree, we respect—even relish—our differences.

A few things for sure though: We love our country, and as before, we'll still put our "lives on the line" to keep it free.

But we don't want to ever again see another "Great Depression!"

Robert F. B. Hansbrough, 2007

Exhibits

I Federal Reserve Banking System as specified by the Federal Reserve Act of 1913.

II Participation of the Blairs & Hansbroughs in the French & Indian Wars & the American Revolution. (Ref. "*Land of Dreams, The Great Adventure.*") © R.F. Hansbrough.

III Major Events & Major Laws Enacted during the Administration of President Woodrow Wilson.

EXHIBIT IA

U.S. FEDERAL Reserve Banking System as Specified by the Federal Reserve Act of 1913

Note: The Federal Reserve Act of 1913 applied only to banks that belonged to the Federal Reserve System. The member banks were divided into three groups.

—Required Reserves—1913—

	Central Reserve Banks City Banks	Reserve City Banks	Country Banks
	25% of total deposits in lawful Money (kept in their own vaults) to cover potential demand withdrawals.	25% of total deposits in lawful money. 50% of this 25% (12½ %) to be kept in their own vaults to cover potential demand withdrawals	15% of total deposits in lawful money. 2/15 of this 15% (6%) to be kept in their own vaults to cover potential demand withdrawals.
Total Deposits	100 % Used for Loans & Investments	100 % Used for Loans & Investments	100 % Used for Loans & Investments
		Allowed Proportions	Allowed Proportions
	Required 25% Reserve in own vaults in lawful money	*Kept 12 ½ % elsewhere	*9% In approved other places

		12 ½ % in own vaults	6% In own vaults
		Req'd. 25% of total deposits in lawful money	Req'd. 15% of total deposits in lawful money

* Disastrous Pyramiding of Bank Demand Deposit Reserves. (See Sheets #IA-2 & IA-3)

EXHIBIT IB

The Pyramidal Of Bank Demand Deposit Reserves

THE FOLLOWING is a brief analysis of the disastrous intra-bank pyramiding practices of bank demand deposit reserves that were ultimately primarily responsible for the "bank crash" of 1929 and the following ten-year (1929-1939) "Great Depression."

The Federal Reserve Act of 1912 was enacted by congress and signed by President Calvin Coolidge to improve the control of the notoriously decentralized U.S. Banking system, bring greater security to depositors and provide greater credit "elasticity" (more or less money in our economic system) as conditions required.

The U.S. Federal Reserve System was their vehicle to carry out the mandates and put the new centralized system into effect.

The Federal Reserve Act specified reserve requirements of the member banks and oversaw their activities.

Of particular concern, and importance, were the always tenuous demand deposits—those deposits that must be paid in "lawful money" (in cash) immediately upon the demands of depositors, mo matter how untimely or financially embarrassing!

If the money wasn't on hand, and the customer was adamant, that was it! "You had it"; Lock your door and go home; you (the bank) were out of business!

Over all, the system worked quite well and was widely accepted, but "the devil was in the details."

EXHIBIT IB (CONTINUED)

The Pyramidal of Band Demand Deposit Reserves (Continued)

IT'S DISCOVERED lack of adequate control over the sequential transfer of required "demand deposit reserves" from bank to bank (interest earnings for the transferring bank; working capital for the receiving bank: and demand deposit reserves for both), had the undesirable net effect in that the greater the number of banks there would be in a specific reserve fund transfer/deposit sequence, the less demand deposit reserve protection there would be for all!

And, for those initially involved, and for the welfare of the millions of unsuspecting other people in the rest of the nation who were enjoying the best of times—ever—the chickens of inattention and the "leave it to the other guy" indifference were about to come home. And there would be a "great awakening!"

EXHIBIT IIA

Participation of the Blairs & Hansbroughs in the French & Indian Wars & the American Revolution. (Ref. "*Land of Dreams, The Great Adventure—An American Saga.*") © R.F. Hansbrough.

Dates & Pages in Manuscript	Details
1742 (p 50)	Alexander Blair enlists in the John Smith Company of the Augusta County Militia (in the Shenandoah Valley).
1750 (p 99)	Col. Wm. Hansbrough (Back in Amherst Co. Virginia) counselled his riflemen of the 1st Virginia Volunteers that much was at stake… "Every shot must count."
1750 (p 100)	Thirty-five year old Alexander Blair of the Augusta County Militia was prepared to stand up & fight… and soon, when they grew up, four of his young sons would follow: In 1758 Capt. William ("Will) Blair Sr. in Augusta County Militia (wounded at Point Pleasant that year). In 1758 John Blair in Augusta County Militia In 1758 James Blair in Augusta County Militia In 1758 Sgt. Samuel Blair in Augusta County Militia (Killed at the Waxhaws, S.C. in massacre by legions of [Banastre Tarleton] in 1780 while serving with Buford).
1754 (p 126)	110 Virginia Volunteers under Captains Robert Stobo and Andrew Lewis, and a company of Oneida Indians under Captain Andrew Montour, finally made it through to great meadows (to be with Washington at Fort Necessity).
1754 (p 135/136)	In Virginia, the volunteers of Amherst and Augusta counties, as in the others, stepped up their practice, and the Hansbrough's and the Blair's and the Cabell's and the Ward's and their many comrades took steps to make sure that their families would be looked after—"just in case."
1755 (p 138-139)	Near Staunton in the Shenandoah Valley, Alexander Blair said Goodbye to Jane and their strangely quiet children (Will, John & James would enlist in the Augusta County Militia in 1758. Samuel would enlist in the 12th Virginia Regiment under Col. Charles Lewis in the same year).

1755 (p 139)	Near Ruckers Run off the Buffalo River in nearby Amherst County, Col. Wm. Hansbrough was also saying his goodbyes to his wife Keziah and their growing young family.
1st May, 1755 (p 141)	Col. Wm. Hansbrough of the Amherst County Volunteers and Alexander Blair of the Augusta County Volunteers congregate at Wills Creek with other Virginia Volunteers to await the coming of Gen. Braddock and his forces prior to marching north to try to take Fort Duquesne (& Braddock's disastrous defeat and his death).
July 9, 1755	Gen. Braddock's forces are ambushed in the Turtle Creek Valley near French Fort Duquesne. Braddock and more than 300 of his army die. Col. Hansbrough & Alexander Blair and their flanking out-rider contingents fight their way back with the rest of the survivors.
Summer 1768 (p 169)	Alexander Blair dies at Staunton; "Will" Blair is now a Captain in the Militia
1773 (p 187)	Capt. Thomas. Buford and his 44 crack riflemen from Bedford County arrive at Staunton to join up with Lewis and other colonial contingents, for the march to fight the Indians at Point Pleasant, and set up camp several days later.

EXHIBIT IIIA

Major Events & Major Laws Enacted During the Administration of President Woodrow Wilson (1913-1921)

1913	Amendment XVI U.S. Constitution (Previously proposed by President Howard Taft.) "The Congress shall have the power to levy and collect taxes on incomes, from whatever source derived, without apportionment among the several states, and without regard to any census or enumeration."
1913	Amendment XVII U.S. Constitution (Previously proposed by President Howard Taft.) "The Senate of the United States shall be composed of two senators from each state, elected by the people..." (Senators were previously elected indirectly by State legislation).
1913	U.S. Federal Reserve Act Intended to centralize the control of the "notoriously decentralized U.S. banking system to bring greater security to depositors, and provide greater credit elasticity."
1913	Underwood Tariff Act Intended to reduce "protectionism" by removing duties previously designed to protect industrial "vested interests" and thus reduce prices "for many."
1913	Franklin Delano Roosevelt appointed as Under Secretary of the U.S. Navy (under Secretary of Navy Joseph Daniels).
1914	Clayton Anti-Trust Act Supplemented the Sherman Anti-Trust Act. Increased market competition. [Exempted some unions from anti-trust provisions.]
1914	Federal Trade Commission established (F.T.C.) Intended to investigate business practices, control monopolistic practices in mislabeling, frustrate business retail fix-pricing combinations, expose false claims of patents, demanded annual corporate reports.

1916	Adamson Act Introduced the eight-hour day. It was originally designed to prevent a railroad strike, but other industries "picked it up" and it became a "benchmark" for industry.
1916	Federal Farm Loan Act Created cheap agricultural credits
1919	President Woodrow Wilson awarded the Nobel Prize for Peace.

EXHIBIT IV

First Inagural Address Franklin Delano Roosevelt, March 4, 1933[23*]

PRESIDENT HOOVER, Mr. Chief Justice, my friends. This is a day of national consecration, and I am certain that my fellow Americans expect that on my induction into the Presidency I will address them with a candor and a decision which the present situation of our Nation impels.

This is pre-eminently the time to speak the truth, the whole truth, frankly and boldly. Nor need we shrink from honestly facing conditions in our country today. This great Nation will endure as it has endured, will revive and will prosper.

So, first of all, let me assert my firm belief that the only thing we have to fear is fear itself—nameless, unreasoning, unjustified terror which paralyzes needed efforts to convert retreat into advance.

In every dark hour of our national life a leadership of frankness and vigor has met with that understanding and support of the people themselves which is essential to victory. I am convinced that you will again give that support to leadership in these critical days.

In such a spirit on my part and on yours we face our common difficulties. They concern, thank God, only material things. Values have shrunken to fantastic levels; taxes have risen; our ability to pay has fallen; government of all kinds is faced by serious curtailment of income; the means of exchange are frozen in the currents of trade; the

---

23* Please refer to "Documents of American History" by Henry Steele [Commager} (1998) pgs 419-422.

withered leaves of industrial enterprise lie on every side; farmers find no markets for their produce; the savings of many years in thousands of families are gone.

More important, a host of unemployed citizens face the grim problem of existence, and an equally great number toil with little return. Only a foolish optimist can deny the dark realities of the moment.

Yet our distress comes from no failure of substance. We are stricken by no plague of locusts. Compared with the perils which our forefathers conquered because they believed and were not afraid, we have still much to be thankful for. Nature still offers her bounty and human efforts have multiplied it. Plenty is at our doorstep, but a generous use of it languishes in the very sight of the supply.

Primarily this is because the rulers of the exchange of mankind's goods have failed, through their own stubbornness and their own incompetence, have admitted their failure, and abdicated. Practices of the unscrupulous money changers stand indicted in the court of public opinion, rejected by the hearts and minds of men.

True they have tried, but their efforts have been cast in the pattern of an outworn tradition. Faced by failure of credit they have proposed only the lending of more money.

Stripped of the lure of profit by which to induce our people to follow their false leadership, they have resorted to exhortations, pleading tearfully for restored confidence. They know only the rules of a generation of self-seekers. They have no vision, and when there is no vision the people perish.

The money changers have fled from their high seats in the temple of our civilization. We may now restore that temple to the ancient truths. The measure of the restoration lies in the extent to which we apply social values more noble than mere monetary profit.

Happiness lies not in the mere possession of money; it lies in the joy of achievement, in the thrill of creative effort.

The joy and moral stimulation of work no longer must be forgotten in the mad chase of evanescent profits. These dark days will be worth all they cost us if they teach us that our true destiny is not to be ministered unto but to minister to ourselves and to our fellow men.

Recognition of the falsity of material wealth as the standard of success goes hand in hand with the abandonment of the false belief that public office and high political position are to be valued only by the standards of pride of place and personal profit; and there must be an end to a conduct in banking and in business which too often has given to a sacred trust the likeness of callous and selfish wrong-doing.

Small wonder that confidence languishes, for it thrives only on honesty, on honor, on the sacredness of obligations, on faithful protection, on unselfish performance; without them it cannot live.

Restoration calls, however, not for changes in ethics alone. This Nation asks for action, and action now.

Our greatest primary task is to put people to work. This is no unsolvable problem if we face it wisely and courageously.

It can be accomplished in part by direct recruiting by the Government itself, treating the task as we would treat the emergency of a war, but at the same time, through this employment, accomplishing greatly needed projects to stimulate and reorganize the use of our natural resources.

Hand in hand with this we must frankly recognize the overbalance of population in our industrial centers and, by engaging on a national scale in a redistribution, endeavor to provide a better use of the land for those best fitted for the land. The task can be helped by definite efforts to raise the values of agricultural products and with this the power to purchase the output of our cities.

It can be helped by preventing realistically the tragedy of the growing loss through foreclosure of our small homes and our farms.

It can be helped by insistence that the Federal, State, and local governments act forthwith on the demand that their cost be drastically reduced.

It can be helped by the unifying of relief activities which today are often scattered, uneconomical, and unequal. It can be helped by national planning for and supervision of all forms of transportation and of communications and other utilities which have a definitely public character.

There are many ways in which it can be helped, but it can never be helped merely by talking about it. We must act and act quickly.

Finally, in our progress toward a resumption of work we require two safeguards against a return of the evils of the old order; there must be a strict supervision of all banking and credits and investments; there must be an end to speculation with other people's money, and there must be provision for an adequate but sound currency.

There are the lines of attack. I shall presently urge upon a new Congress in special session detailed measures for their fulfillment, and I shall seek the immediate assistance of the several States.

Through this program of action we address ourselves to putting our own national house in order and making income balance outgo.

Our international trade relations, though vastly important, are in point of time and necessity secondary to the establishment of a sound national economy.

I favor as a practical policy the putting of first things first. I shall spare no effort to restore world trade by international economic readjustment, but the emergency at home cannot wait on that accomplishment.

The basic thought that guides these specific means of national recovery is not narrowly nationalistic.

It is the insistence, as a first consideration, upon the interdependence of the various elements in all parts of the United States—a recognition of the old and permanently important manifestation of the American spirit of the pioneer.

It is the way to recovery. It is the immediate way. It is the strongest assurance that the recovery will endure.

In the field of world policy I would dedicate this Nation to the policy of the good neighbor—the neighbor who resolutely respects himself and, because he does so, respects the rights of others—the neighbor who respects his obligations and respects the sanctity of his agreements in and with a world of neighbors.

If I read the temper of our people correctly, we now realize as we have never realized before our interdependence on each other; that we can not merely take but we must give as well; that if we are to go forward, we must move as a trained and loyal army willing to sacrifice for the good of a common discipline, because without such discipline no progress is made, no leadership becomes effective.

We are, I know, ready and willing to submit our lives and property to such discipline, because it makes possible a leadership which aims at a larger good.

This I propose to offer, pledging that the larger purposes will bind upon us all as a sacred obligation with a unity of duty hitherto evoked only in time of armed strife.

With this pledge taken, I assume unhesitatingly the leadership of this great army of our people dedicated to a disciplined attack upon our common problems.

Action in this image and to this end is feasible under the form of government which we have inherited from our ancestors.

Our Constitution is so simple and practical that it is possible always to meet extraordinary needs by changes in emphasis and arrangement without loss of essential form.

That is why our constitutional system has proved itself the most superbly enduring political mechanism the modern world has produced. It has met every stress of vast expansion of territory, of foreign wars, of bitter internal strife, of world relations.

It is to be hoped that the normal balance of executive and legislative authority may be wholly adequate to meet the unprecedented task before us. But it may be that an unprecedented demand and need for undelayed action may call for temporary departure from that normal balance of public procedure.

I am prepared under my constitutional duty to recommend the measures that a stricken nation in the midst of a stricken world may require.

These measures, or such other measures as the Congress may build out of its experience and wisdom, I shall seek, within my constitutional authority, to bring to speedy adoption.

But in the event that the Congress shall fail to take one of these two courses, and in the event that the national emergency is still critical, I shall not evade the clear course of duty that will then confront me.

I shall ask the Congress for the one remaining instrument to meet the crisis—broad Executive power to wage a war against the emergency, as great as the power that would be given to me if we were in fact invaded by a foreign foe.

For the trust reposed in me I will return the courage and the devotion that befit the time. I can do no less.

We face the arduous days that lie before us in the warm courage of the national unity; with the clear consciousness of seeking old and precious moral values; with the clean satisfaction that comes from the stern performance of duty by old and young alike. We aim at the assurance of a rounded and permanent national life.

We do not distrust the future of essential democracy. The people of the United States have not failed. In their need they have registered a mandate that they want direct, vigorous action.

They have asked for discipline and direction under leadership. They have made me the present instrument of their wishes. In the spirit of the gift I take it.

In this dedication of a Nation we humbly ask the blessing of God. May He protect each and every one of us. May He guide me in the days to come.

EXHIBIT V

Desperate Journey When We Were Young & The Great Depression

Bibliography

Cathcart, Brian. "The Fly in the Cathedral."
New York: Farrar, Straus and Giroux, 2005

Burns, A.E. and Neil, A.C. and Watson, D.S., "Modern Economics."
New York: Harcourt, Bruce and Co. 1948.

David Crystal (ed.). "Biographical Encyclopedia."
Cambridge: University Press, 1998.

Fink, Donald G. and Beatty, H.W. "Standard Handbook for Electrical Engineers." (11th ed).
New York: McGraw-Hill Inc. 1978, pp 515/528

Fischer, David H. "The Great Wave, Price Revolutions and the Rhythm of History."
Oxford: Oxford University Press, 1999.

Friedel, Frank. "Franklin D. Roosevelt, A Rendezvous with Destiny."
New York, N.Y.: Back Bay Books/Little Brain and Co., 1990.

Gammill, P.F., "Fundamentals of Economics," 4th ed.
New York and London: Harper Brothers, 1943.

Johnson, Paul. "A History of the American People."
New York: Harper Collins, 1997.

Kent, Raymond P., "Money and Banking," Revised (ed).
New York and Toronto: Reinhart and Co. Inc., 1951.

Mund, V.A. "Government and Business."
New York: Harper and Brothers, 1950.

Smith, Adam, "Wealth of Nations."
New York: Promethius Books, 1991.

Commager, Henry Steele (ed.), "Documents of American History," Fourth Edition.
New York and London: Appleton-Century-Crofts, Inc. 1948.

Bonneville, Joseph Howard and Lloyd Ellis Dewey, "Organizing and Financing Business." Fifth Edition.
New York: Prentice-Hall Inc., 1953.

Hyne, Norman. Ph.D. "Petroleum Geology, Exploration, Drilling and Production", 2nd Ed.
Tulsa, Oklahoma: Penwell Corp., 2001.

Pearce, Pred. "With Speed And Violence," 1st Ed., Boston, Mass: Beacon Press, 2007.

Simmons, Matthew, R. "Twilight In The Desert," 1st Edition.
Hoboken, New Jersey: John Wiley and Sons Inc., 2005.

About the Author (Who am I?)

AT THE end of most stories, it is customary for authors to write a little sketch of themselves to give readers an image of who they are and lend credence to what they say.

*Now that the main st*ory in this book has come to an end, I would like to leave you with a "thumb-nail" picture of who I am. And, in the process, reveal a little of the background that has impelled and guided me along the way.

Throughout our lives, we have all had dreams and adventures, triumphs and disappointments. Mine, I am sure, have been much like yours. Though the paths we have taken may have differed, our quests for mutual understanding, acceptance and peace of mind are much the same.

And the teachings and lessons learned from heroes and loved ones who came before are indelibly embedded in our character and abetted by the choices we make and opportunities seized.

By heritage I am a "Yankee" from way back. I am very proud of the honest, caring, hardworking ways and commitments of my pioneer forefathers. And all who came with them, to this unspoiled land of promise. And fashioned homes and lives from its ruggedness. And from its beauty, a "can-do" philosophy nearly a century and a half before the beginning of the American Revolution. But I won't go into their names; that would mar the mystique of it all. Suffice it to say that they came from many places: England, Scotland, Ireland – even a few from the Netherlands and France. And, oh yes, many fine relatives from Sweden too. God bless them. I love them all!

In preceding chapters I have already mentioned quite a lot about my family background. To say more would be pretty redundant and would add little, if anything, to the story. So I won't go into that any further.

I do feel it appropriate, though, that I tell you a little about my scholastic and "working" background so that you can judge for yourself the veracity of some of the more technical subjects and conclusions I have written about.

That said, here goes: I'll try to be brief and to the point as much as possible!

It all started out in the late Spring of 1942 when I had just graduated from High School (Traverse City, Michigan) and was a recently enlisted "apprentice seaman" at the Great Lakes Naval Training Center "Boot Camp" near Chicago, Illinois.

I had just been given my choice of Navy Schools. At Dad's suggestion I chose electrical. This was the last time I would see him alive; he died a few months later.

Then "Boot Camp" soon over, it was off to the new naval training facility at Iowa State College, Ames, Iowa. And a berth with three other fledgling "shipmates" in a room of the new "Friley Hall".

From then on, it's all history; my training had served me well, and two warships later and a number of "engagements" with the enemy, I ended up one day as one of the "chiefs" in the "E" division (electrical) of one of the largest battleships[24] in the world.

And, in time, the war was suddenly over. And I was a "civilian" again.

Then it was off to college under the new "G.I." Bill (what a lifesaver that was!). And just as it had been for so many young lads and lassies in those days, recently returned from the ravages of the war (and with vivid memories of the "Great Depression" too), this was my one big chance! The hoped-for way to a better tomorrow was suddenly

---

[24]* Fleet Mine Sweeper, U.S.S. Motive (AM-102) – Aleutian Islands, and Battleship U.S.S. Wisconsin (BB-64) – South Pacific

there before me. And it's name was "knowledge" and "understanding". And I and many other new "veterans" of "the war" jumped to its finding with a passion.

And in time a brand new generation of professionals and specialists of all description was born. And the worn-out ranks of the mothers and fathers, sisters and brothers who had labored so hard to build the ships and planes and implements of war began to be replenished by the eager-to-get-going ranks of those who had just returned.

And we set to work with the enthusiasm of youth and a great desire to learn all we could, make the necessary choices, and get going. It was a fast-moving world out there. We'd been away a long time. And we had to catch up fast!

So we traded a world of bugles and battles for a new world of books and lectures and labs and the "burning of the midnight oil" to discover our options and learn all we could in the fields of endeavor that interested us most.

And wouldn't you just know: mine was engineering. And, being a curious fellow, I was interested in the gyrations of the economy too; and in the intricacies of the law and the rationale and piroettes of its man-made rules and regulations that surround us. But, "What the heck!" I was young; the world was "my oyster"; the challenge of a wide-open, wonderful world was there before me! So I went back to school to learn what I could of them all[25]. And in time, the years did go by. And my darling wife, Clarice, was there by my side to hold my hand; and guide me; and give me courage. And now she's in heaven and waiting. And I miss her so! And I'm suddenly old. The bloom of

[25]* Engineering: (Studies at the University of Michigan and the Detroit Institute of Technology – "D.I.T.", and P.E. Licence from the state of New Hampshire)

• Business Administration: Studies at "D.I.T" with a B.B.A. in Industrial Management.

• Studies of Law:

• Pre-Law at Detroit Institute of Technology ("D.I.T."); Law School at the Detroit College of Law.

youth is gone, and God willing, we'll be together again soon.

In days gone by, both the Detroit Institute of Technology and the Detroit College of Law were conveniently located near each other. Just off Grand Circus Park, in (then) "downtown" Detroit.

Many officials of Detroit and nearby cities, and executives of the Ford Motor Company were graduates of one or the other (and often both).

As I mentioned earlier, Henry Ford Sr. built his first car in a nearby shed. And taught classes in "blacksmithing" to "D.I.T." students in the 1890's.

The atmosphere at both (particularly at D.I.T.), though business-like and "to the point" was quite informal and relaxing. I enjoyed many after-class chats with Professor Smith (economics) who had been a labor-management "trouble shooter" for President Harding in his administration.

Often in the evenings, before the start of night school classes, my professor of "money and banking" (and other finance courses), who was also an executive of the Detroit National Bank, often had supper with me in the dining room of the nearby YWCA. We shared many interesting (sometimes amusing) talks together. One in particular stands out in memory. It was about a little "run-in" I recently had with the instructor of my summer-time "History of American Political Parties" classes. For propriety I'll just refer to him as Mr. "I.P" (ire provoker). It went something like this: Mr. "I.P." had just finished reading aloud a beautiful tribute to the American way of life written by Malcolm Bingay, one of my favorite authors. Then slamming down the paper, he turned to our class and shouted out loud: "What utter trash: what do we have to lose?" Stunned by his "un-American" comments, I shouted out loud: "Nothing but our chains" (a repetition of a well-known anti-everything comment by Karl Marx in his "Communist Manifesto"). Utter silence filled the room. Then turning to me – and the stunned class – Mr. "I.P." shouted back, "One more comment like that, Mr. Hansbrough, and I'll throw you out of class." Angered even more I returned the compliment and replied: "It will take more than you to do it!" A month or so later, when summer classes were over, I stopped by the registrar's office to check on the status of my remaining required credits for graduation. I was particularly interested in my grade for the recent History of American Political Parties course. My thesis for the course concentrated on the American Westward Movement. On reviewing my credits for the course, the registrar announced in surprise: "Why, Mr. Hansbrough, you got an 'A'!" Then, surprisingly, another voice from the nearby archives "chimed-in": "But he had to work for it." It was Mr. "I.P." – he had been listening!

Long years have now passed. I never did get that thesis back. "Mr. I.P." had been studying for his doctorate at a well-known mid-west University. You don't think? Naah, he couldn't have used it that way.

Now is the time in this section about "the author" to make a few comments about what I feel I have accomplished or tried to do in my working life.

On-the-job experience and knowledge, gained through structured academic regimens of study, "by the books", have played big parts.

But first, please indulge me, if you will, while I make a few personal comments on what I believe to be the meanings and relationships of the terms: "education", "knowledge", and "awareness".

("Sandy" and "Peggy" please bear with me, and forgive me, as Claire would do, if I err in interpretation and am wrong).

Here goes:

The term, "awareness" is a key part of this discussion. "Knowledge" is essentially an acquired awareness of real and potential stimuli that exist in the world all around.

The term "education" has at least a two-fold meaning: on one hand, it can refer to the extent of acquired awareness. On the other hand, it often refers to the ways and means (the "highways and byways" we take) to learn and become aware.

I'll get off this subject real soon! But what I would like to suggest is that education comes in many guises! There is a hard way called getting it through experience; and there's another hard way called "burning the midnight oil" and "getting it through the books".

Both of these ways work. Neither should be derided. The important thing is to get that education; get that knowledge. And put the good parts learned into practice.

What are the "good parts"? Well I won't venture into that one! I'll leave it to you. But, among other things, it deals with desires, expectations, law, and religion in an honorable, respectful way.

Now! Just what did I do? Well, it's a rather long story. But a theme of sorts, rather runs through it. I'll try to be brief.

I am sure you have already surmised by now, Engineering, particularly in the electrical field, has played a big part in my working life. And so did Business Administration. Particularly in the automotive, maritime and related and associated industries.

From that day that I first began my electrical training for the Navy at Iowa State College at Ames, Iowa, in the fall of 1942, to the time I said my last good-bye to fellow engineers at the Navy Subase at Bangor, Washington, 45 years later, I have enjoyed the thrill of new discovery, the excitement in the development of new approaches and new techniques. And the pride and satisfaction in just keeping things going – often under difficult circumstances.

But, best of all, I have enjoyed the friendship and comraderie of many wonderful, caring people along the way who have striven real hard throughout their lives to quietly – often unnoticed – make a real difference and "lighten the load" of us all.

As has been the case for most in my profession I have gone to many meetings and conferences held in many parts of the country[26] which were sponsored (and usually chaired) by manufacturers, government entities (regional, state, and national) and professional organizations

[26]* For me, a number of conferences in near-by Canada too.

(often my own, "A.I.E.E.") to keep us abreast of latest developments[27], review the "state of the art", discuss legal and operational challenges, and obtain our "input".

When it came to new development, I was often called upon to discuss what I had done in "demand control" and other things I was doing in the energy "savings" field. For me, it was "heady times"; I felt that I was in the forefront of new developments – new challenges. And, to be real honest, it was exhilarating to feel that I was finally doing my little part.

[27] * Features and projects discussed included: manufacturing plant design, power source adequacy, transmission lines, substations, systems control coordination, cost control, and energy control and use reduction.

The Greatest Depression of All

About twenty-five years ago, when I was the Chief Electrical Engineer of a high-energy-use steel-making company in the "Northwest", a vice president of my company and I were invited to attend a three-day conference at the "Jacktar Hotel" (across from the "Forum" in Los Angeles) on the status of all known energy sources in our country, and in the world. And on the known or estimated "reserves".

It was a meeting I will never forget: not only for the profoundly disturbing, well-supported revelations that our fast-diminishing supplies of un-renewable fuel of all kinds (solid carbonates, such as coal; hydrocarbons such as petroleum) were running out fast and that the "reserves" we had been counting on simply weren't there, but for the feeling that there was little we could do about it except search for possible alternatives.

But assembled, all around, were the scientists and professionals and engineers who had worked real hard to define the problem. And we left with strong "roll-up our sleeves" feeling of commitment to find the answers. But, in all honesty, they haven't been found yet.

But another big problem has intrusively "come to the fore". And its significance and threatening impact on the world and all living beings on it is huge: almost beyond imagination! And it comes under many and various names: "Global warming", "climate tipping point", "end of the world", etc., etc! And we have heard about it so often in so many ways and under so many names that we have seemingly lost its terrible significance.

Think back to the time, 65 million years ago, "when a giant comet or meteorite slammed into the earth off the tip of the Yucatan Peninsula of Mexico and "wiped-out" all the Dinosaurs and flying reptiles. And 75% of all species of plants and animals. And the earth was thrown into total darkness for many months"[28]. Reading this, I believe, will give us all a feeling of the huge impact that changes in the climate of our planet could very well bring to us all!

Should these warnings be taken seriously? You (and I) better believe it!

[28]* The time of the "Great Killing", ref. pg. 47 "Petroleum Geology, Exploration, Drilling and Production" by Norman J. Hyne, Ph.D., 2nd Ed., 2001.

In closing, I want to say I have met and become friends with many wonderful people along the way.

Among them was Robert A. Smith, one time head of the George Washington Carver Laboratory of the Ford Motor Company.

Bob was a personal friend of Henry Ford Sr. founder of the Ford Motor Company. Both had connections with Detroit Institute of Technology (D.I.T.) just as did I.

Henry Ford built his first automobile a few blocks away. And in his "spare time" taught classes in "Blacksmithing" at D.I.T. in the 1890's.

Bob graduated from there with a degree in Chemistry in the middle of the 1940's. My degree, in Industrial Management, came from there in 1956.

Bob had a never-ending streak of adventure in him just like me. And we sailed together many times on my sailboats, all with the name "Clarice." Sometimes on the Great Lakes, other times up and down the coasts of British Columbia. He was an interesting, wonderful companion.

And he grew up as a poor boy too. On our trips to the North Country, we used to talk about things of the past a lot, and muse on the beauty of the scenes all around.

Two of his best remembered remarks are very pertinent to the theme of this story and are an appropriate ending:

Once on a batten-breaking stormy night sail down the riled-up Detroit River, Bob leaned over to my brave little daughter Beth and consolingly remarked, "Sure beats sitting at home reading about it in a rocking chair, doesn't it!"

Another time, at anchor in a far away secluded cove he turned to me and mused aloud, "Bob," he said, "Things sure didn't turn out too badly for two poor boys form the Great Depression, did they?"

And I answered aloud (and in my heart), "That's for sure dear friend; we made a good try."

Robert F.B. Hansbrough
2007

EPILOG

"Desperate Journey – When We Were Young & The Great Depression"

In a way, this book is a "ballad of yesterday, today and tomorrow." And in carrying on with the theme of Vera Brittain's beautiful book, "Testament to Youth," this is also a testament to the legacy of love and caring and sharing of those who have gone before; and is a challenge to we who are left to carry on in their quest for a better today and tomorrow. But to win that goal, we must recognize and understand our adversaries. I have tried, in this book (sometimes by example; other times by inuendo) to point out who those adversaries are.

But, you know, there is more than a little truth to the sometimes quoted statement, "I have met the enemy and the enemy is me."

Take economics, for example. It is really little more than the study of human behavior in response to perceived wants and needs, and of our actions and interactions to meet defined financial well-being goals–"Cause and effect" pure and simple–but rashness, carelessness, impropriety, selfishness and greed play a big part in upsetting the balance. "Left alone," as in the precepts of "laisse faire," their ugliness has no place to hide. And, without the sustenance of self-serving, non-competitive forces will quickly disappear into oblivion.

As I have mentioned earlier in this book: An economy is like a delicate heirloom watch: hold it carefully! Don't wind it too tight! It can be easily broken!

Robert F.B. Hansbrough

www.ingramcontent.com/pod-product-compliance
Ingram Content Group UK Ltd.
Pitfield, Milton Keynes, MK11 3LW, UK
UKHW021053270726
13967UKWH00012B/635

9 781425 122553